LADY GUNSMITH

8

Roxy Doyle and the Silver Queen

Books by J.R. Roberts
(Robert J. Randisi)

Lady Gunsmith series
The Legend of Roxy Doyle
The Three Graves of Roxy Doyle
Roxy Doyle and The Shanghai Saloon
Roxy Doyle and The Traveling Circus Show
The Portrait of Gavin Doyle
Roxy Doyle and the Desperate Housewife
Roxy Doyle and the James Boys
Roxy Doyle and the Silver Queen

The Gunsmith series

Angel Eyes series

Tracker series

Mountain Jack Pike series

Coming Soon!
Lady Gunsmith 9
Roxy Doyle and the Lady Executioner

For more information visit:
www.SpeakingVolumes.us

LADY GUNSMITH

8

Roxy Doyle and the Silver Queen

J.R. Roberts

SPEAKING VOLUMES, LLC
NAPLES, FLORIDA
2019

Roxy Doyle and the Silver Queen

ISBN 978-1-64540-132-2

Chapter One

Roxy Doyle was impressed as she rode into Leadville.

All she knew about the place was that there had been a gold strike there over ten years before. But it had played out fairly quickly. Riding in she was expecting to see a worn-out town made up mostly of tents and shacks. Instead, she found herself in a growing and thriving city, with tall buildings, paved streets, and blocks of new stores.

She also saw two incredible 3-story buildings, one of which was the Tabor Opera House, and the other with a sign that said The Tabor Grand Hotel. The hotel looked like it would be the lap of luxury, but Roxy's pockets were far from bulging with money, and she knew she would never be able to afford a room there.

So she continued to ride until she found what looked like a more affordable hotel. It was two stories, and on a block of older buildings, more like the ones she expected to find.

She reined in her horse in front, tied it off and went inside. There was hardly any lobby to it, just a front desk next to a set of stairs that led up.

The clerk's eyes widened when he chose to look up at her. They looked watery behind thick glasses. He had sparse hair, but still appeared to be in his twenties.

"Can I help you, Ma'am?" he asked.

"I need a room."

"Of course," he said, "although there are nicer hotels in town you could stay at."

"You're trying to talk me out of staying here?"

"Ma'am," he said, "you're so beautiful I just think you'd fit in better at one of those other places."

"How much are your rooms?" she asked.

"A dollar a night," he said.

"I'll fit in here just fine," she said. "Can I sign in?"

"Sure."

He turned the register around so she could sign it, then handed her a key.

"Right at the top of the stairs," he said.

"I'd like something in the middle," she countered, "not by the stairs, and not overlooking the street."

"Of course." He took the key back and gave her another one. "There you go."

"Thank you."

"Can I do somethin' else for you?" he asked. "Take care of your horse?"

"Is there a livery stable nearby?" she asked.

"Just down the street," he said. "It's cheap, but Andy will do the job."

"All right," she said, "that would be kind of you. I'll go get my rifle and saddlebags."

She went outside, collected her things and then returned.

"Let me know when it's done," she said.

"Yes, Miss Doyle."

She went up the stairs, found her door and entered the room. It wasn't particularly clean, but she had been in dirtier ones. She dropped her saddlebags onto the bed and leaned her rifle against the wall next to it. Then she sat and bounced on the mattress. It was kind of flabby. The bed springs squeaked, but it would be better than sleeping on the ground.

She went to the window and peered out, saw that she was looking down at the roof of the building next door. But there was a space between the two buildings—not an alley, but enough to insure no one could get to her window.

Satisfied that her room was unreachable, she started for the door, intending to find herself a cheap but good meal. Before she reached the door, however, there was a knock. When she opened it, the clerk stood there. His hands were empty, but he had obviously combed his hair, and applied what smelled like lilac water to his cheeks.

“Your horse is in the livery, Miss,” he said. “It’ll be well taken care of.”

“What’s your name?” she asked him.

“Henry, Miss.” She noticed she’d gone from “Ma’am” to “Miss.”

“Well, thank you, Henry,” she said, “you’ve been real sweet.”

“If you need anything else, just let me know,” Henry said. “I’ll be on duty all night.”

“I’ll remember that,” she said. “In fact, you can help me with something. I’m looking for a good meal that won’t cost me a fortune.”

“I know just the place,” he told her, “and if you tell ’em I sent ya, you’ll get a better price.”

“Sounds like just the place,” she said.

***

She followed Henry’s directions until she was standing in front of a place called Dexter’s Café. Henry told her Dexter was his cousin, and reinforced that she should mention his name.

She didn’t waste any time. As soon as she entered and a waiter approached her, she said, “Henry sent me over.”

The man made a face. “You stayin’ in that fleabag Roadside Hotel?”

“Is that the name?” she asked. “I didn’t see that anywhere, but it’ll do for now.”

“Well, anyway,” he said, “you came to the right place to eat. Follow me.”

He led her across the floor of the half-filled room to a table that sat among other, occupied tables.

“How about that one?” she asked, pointing to a table by the back wall.

“Sure,” he said, “anything for a friend of Henry’s.”

As she sat, she asked, “Are you Dexter, his cousin?”

“Nope, Dexter’s in the kitchen,” he said, “but we waiters know to treat Henry’s friends good. Can I recommend somethin’?”

“Something that won’t cost me a fortune?” she asked.

“Don’t worry about that, Miss,” he said. “A woman who looks like you shouldn’t never have to pay for her own meal.”

“All right, then,” she said. “Whatever you recommend.”

As he hurried back to the kitchen, she wondered what she might have gotten herself into?

Chapter Two

The food turned out to be pretty good.

The waiter brought her out a plate of chicken and vegetables. While it looked rather plain, it turned out to be bursting with flavors.

"So?" he asked, when she was finished. "What did you think?"

"It was delicious," she said. "Thank you."

"Some dessert?"

"Why not? Bring me something good."

He went to the kitchen and returned with a bowl of blueberry cobbler, and a cup of coffee.

"Enjoy," he said.

And she did. By the time she was finished she was quite satisfied with her meal. Now all that remained was to pay for it.

When he brought her the check, she looked at him and said, "You're kidding."

"Too much?"

"Fifty cents?" she asked. "For all that?"

"That's what Dexter said."

"Can I meet Dexter and thank him?" she asked.

"Dexter's kind of . . . odd," the waiter said. "He doesn't like to meet the customers."

"Well then, will you tell him for me how good everything was?" she said.

"I'll tell him."

The place had filled up a bit more while she was eating, so when she stood and walked out, she was the center of attention. She knew it was because of her looks. She didn't mind. In fact, she preferred it to people watching her because they knew who she was.

***

She decided to wash the meal down with a beer, at a saloon. And for that she decided to try one of the better ones rather than the cheaper. After all, she hadn't spent much for her room, or her meal.

A few doors down from the Grand Hotel she found a place called the Silver Dollar Saloon. As she entered, she saw a modest mahogany bar, with footrails and spittoons that looked like brass. As she approached the bar, she felt the eyes of the other customers following her.

"Beer," she said to the bartender.

"Nope."

"What do you mean, no?"

"You want the back bar," he said.

"And why is that?"

"Lady," the grizzled old bartender said, "somebody who looks like you should be drinkin' over there."

He pointed toward the back of the room.

"Does the beer cost more back there?" she asked, suspiciously.

"The first one'll be on the house," the man said.

"Well, in that case . . ." she said, and pushed away from the bar.

When she got to the back, she saw that the bar there was made of white oak, and behind it were three quarters of an inch diamond dust mirrors. In addition, she was surprised to recognize the bartender who, at that moment, was cleaning glasses with a towel. As she approached, he watched her with no indication that he also recognized her.

"Hi, Doc," she said.

"Roxy Doyle," Doc Holliday said. "What are you doin' here?"

"I was about to ask you the same thing."

"Things got hot in Tombstone after the O.K. Corral thing," he said. "I traveled some and found this place. It's growing, but it's a quiet place to live."

"I'm just passing through," she said.

"Still lookin' for your father?"

She nodded, but didn't want to discuss it because the trail had gone so cold.

"The bartender in front said something about the first beer being on the house."

"Comin' up," he said.

He drew a cold mug of beer and set it down in front of her.

"Does this apply to everybody?" she asked, picking it up.

"Only if they look like you," he said, "which means hardly ever."

She sipped the beer, then said, "I wouldn't have expected to find you tending bar."

"I help out when I can," he said. "Usually I'm dealin' faro."

"Ah," she said, "that's more like it."

Roxy had been to Tombstone, met Holliday and the Earps, and left, all before the shootout had occurred. She heard about it later, and was sad to hear of Morgan Earp's death.

Holliday was a blonde man, painfully thin and—as she recalled—very ill. At least at the moment he wasn't coughing up blood.

She watched as he served others, saw that his skill as a bartender might have even matched his skill with cards, or a gun. It was a shame the man was fated to die young.

"Another?" Holliday asked, coming back to her.

"I'm still working on this one. But tell me a bit about Leadville."

"After the gold mines played out, they found the lead, and the town has grown from there. The Matchless Mine is the biggest, and the richest mine owner is Horace Tabor."

"Ah, the man whose name is on the hotel and the opera house," she said.

"Yes," Doc said. "He brought all the materials in from Denver when he had them built."

"Does he live here?"

"He has a house here, and in Denver. He built them for his young bride, Baby Doe."

"Baby Doe?" Roxy asked. "What kind of a name is that?"

"Her real name is Elizabeth. She was married to a man named Doe, before Horace, but I don't know where the 'baby' comes from. I do know one thing."

"What's that?"

"Horace would like you a lot," Doc said. "He's very fond of beautiful women."

"I'll take that as a compliment."

"But Baby Doe, she's gonna hate you."

"And why's that?"

"She's been known as the most beautiful woman in Colorado," Doc said.

"So? What's that got to do with me?"

"Once the men of Leadville and Denver see you," Doc continued in his slight Southern drawl, "she might not hang onto that title for very long. This is gonna be interesting."

"What makes you think I'll even meet Horace and Baby Doe Tabor?" she asked.

"Horace knows everything that goes on in Leadville and Denver," Doc said.

"Then why doesn't he have you working for him in one of his places?" Roxy asked.

Doc laughed.

"He tried, but I'm not for sale. I prefer it here. But you . . . once he hears that Lady Gunsmith is here, and how beautiful you are, he'll make a point of meeting you."

"Now you're laying it on thick, Doc," she said.

"Then there's that quality you have."

"What quality is that?"

He leaned on the bar.

"You don't seem to know how beautiful you really are."

"You know," she said, "it might be interesting to meet Horace and Baby Doe, at that."

"They say when Horace first met Elizabeth, he handed her five thousand dollars."

Now Roxy *was* interested. Five thousand dollars would fund her search for her father for as long as it took.

"Doc," she said, "I think I'll have that second beer now."

Chapter Three

Roxy left the Silver Dollar, promising Doc that she would return later. They had not become good friends during her stay in Tombstone—in fact, she had gotten close to Johnny Ringo—but since he was the only person she knew at the moment in Leadville, they were civil to each other.

From the Silver Dollar she went back to her hotel, where the desk clerk waved to her frantically.

"What is it?" she asked, approaching the desk.

"There's no need for you to go upstairs," the clerk said.

"And why is that?"

"You don't have a room here."

"I did a little while ago," she said. "What's changed?"

"I've been told to inform you that you now have a room at the Grand Hotel."

"The Tabor?"

"That's the only Grand Hotel in Leadville," the clerk said.

"And how did I manage that?" she asked.

"I was wondering the same thing," the clerk said.

"Who told you to give me this message?"

"It was a man from the Hotel."

"And my saddlebags and rifle?"

"They're in your room at the Hotel, Miss."

"I suppose I'll have to go and get them," she said. "Please don't give away my room here. I'll be coming back."

"Don't worry about that," he said. "We have plenty of rooms."

Roxy stepped outside, intending to walk to the Grand Hotel, but, as she did, a small man in his fifties stepped in front of her. He was dressed in a dark suit, a very white shirt, a black bowler hat and a broad smile. From what she could tell, he was not armed.

"Miss Doyle?"

"Yes."

"My name is George Grant. I've been sent to bring you to your hotel."

"This is my hotel."

"I mean, the Grand Hotel. I have a buggy." He waved at a buggy that was parked in front of the hotel.

"I don't have a room at the Grand Hotel," she said. "I can't afford a room at the Grand Hotel."

"That won't be a problem," Grant said. "There won't be any charge for your room. You're to have it, and anything else you need during your stay."

"And by whose authority has all this been arranged?" she asked.

"That would be Mr. Tabor."

"Horace Tabor?"

The man smiled again.

"Yes, he *is* my boss, and I always do what my boss tells me to do."

"And what about the boss's wife?" Roxy asked. "Does she know about this . . . arrangement?"

"Mrs. Tabor is in Denver," he said.

"And Mister Tabor?"

"He's here, in Leadville."

"At the Grand Hotel?"

"No, he has a house here. He doesn't stay at the hotel. That's for guests."

"So when I go to my room at the hotel, I won't find him there?" she asked.

"Oh, no," Grant laughed, "not at all."

"Then why has Mr. Tabor given me a room?" she asked. "In fact, how does he know who I am, and that I'm in town?"

"I think you'll have to ask him all those questions yourself, Miss Doyle," Grant said, "when you see him."

"And when would that be?"

"Tomorrow night, if you're willing."

"Willing to do what?"

"Have supper with him at his house."

"I understand Mrs. Tabor is very beautiful," Roxy said.

"Indeed, she is. She's the most beautiful woman I've ever seen—or, she was."

Roxy didn't ask him to explain that remark.

"All right, Mr. Grant," she said. "If only because I'm curious about this wonderful hotel, let's go for a buggy ride."

Chapter Four

The lobby of Tabor's Grand Hotel was ostentatious, to say the least. Huge, vaulted ceilings with chandeliers hanging from them, tiled floors, dark paneled walls.

As George Grant walked her to the front desk, the tiles turned to luxurious, deep carpet.

"Ah, Mr. Grant," the desk clerk greeted. He was also wearing a dark suit, which Roxy figured may have been a uniform for Tabor's employees. Only he was tall, slender, in his forties, with slicked down black hair and a small mustache.

"Mr. Winston," Grant said, "this is Mr. Tabor's guest, Roxy Doyle."

"Ah, yes," Winston said, looking at Roxy, taking in her red hair, pale skin, and the gun on her hip, "and I can see why."

"Can you?" Roxy asked.

"I didn't mean any offense, Miss," Winston said. "I just happen to know that Mr. Tabor likes beautiful things. If I offended you, allow me to apologize."

"Apology accepted," she said. "Do the rooms have bathtubs?"

"They do," Winston said. "The Grand Hotel has all the modern conveniences."

"Then I'd like to see mine now," she said.

"Of course."

He turned, took a key from the wall behind him, and handed it to her.

"Mr. Grant can see you to your room."

"Thank you." She looked at the key, which had a room number attached to it. "I think I can find it on my own."

"As you wish," Grant said. "I was only tasked with moving you here from that rat trap you were going to stay in."

"Please thank your boss for me," Roxy said, "and tell him I'll see him for supper tomorrow."

"A buggy will be here tomorrow night to take you there," Grant said, tipping his hat to her. "Good-night, Miss Doyle."

"Good-night, Mr. Grant."

The two men watched her as she walked up the broad stairway to the second floor. She walked down a deeply carpeted hallway until she found the door that matched the number on her key, and let herself in. When she turned up the gas lamp on the wall next to the door, she caught her breath. She was in a suite, larger than many houses she had been in. The furnishings were ornate; the carpet matched the thickness of the ones in the lobby and hallway. The curtains were heavy and would keep all the light from the room in the morning, until they were drawn. Everything was in slightly different shades of burgundy.

She walked into the next room, where she found her saddlebags on the large, firm bed, and her rifle in a corner. She walked to a doorway she thought would lead to the indoor facilities, but found it was a closet. She was also surprised to find it packed with clothes—mostly dresses, and gowns. All of the colors would go wonderfully with her red hair.

She closed the closet, went to another doorway on the other side of the room. There she found the bathtub.

She made immediate use of it.

***

After a hot bath, she found a robe in the closet and put it on. It was silk, and more comfortable than any dress she had ever worn. She wouldn't want to get too used to it, though. In her search for her father, this kind of luxury wouldn't last.

She walked to the window and looked out. It overlooked the front of the hotel, but was far enough away from the street that the sound of passing buggies and hansom cabs were not annoying. She was becoming more and more surprised at what Leadville had to offer.

She recalled what Doc Holliday had told her about Tabor's Matchless Mine. She wondered how many other mines and wealthy miners there were in town, and how long Tabor would remain the richest man in Leadville?

She was very curious about how Tabor knew who she was, that she was in town, and what hotel she was in? But it was Doc's comment about the five thousand dollars Tabor had given to his Baby Doe at their first meeting. She certainly wasn't looking to compete with Baby Doe for Tabor's affections, but even a fraction of that five thousand would be helpful to her.

So she was perfectly willing to accept his hospitality in his hotel, and even to have supper with him at his home.

Or to sleep on the firmest, most expensive mattress she had ever experienced.

***

Horace Tabor's black houseman brought George Grant into the rich man's study, where Tabor was sitting, reading. Tabor was in his early fifties, with a receding hairline and a large, handlebar mustache.

"Mr. Grant, sir," the houseman announced.

"Thank you, Solomon," Tabor said. "That'll be all."

"Yes, sir," the man said, and withdrew.

"Well?" Tabor asked Grant.

"She's in her room at your hotel, sir," Grant said.

"Ah, so she accepted the room?"

"Yes, sir, after some . . . persuasion on my part."

"And what about supper tomorrow night?"

"That, too, sir."

"And tell me," Tabor said, leaning forward with great interest, "is she as beautiful as they say?"

"If I may say," Grant replied, "even moreso, sir."

Tabor sat back.

"Then I just hope she also measures up to her reputation with a gun."

"Oh, she wears it quite comfortably, sir," Grant said, "I'd be willing to venture a guess and say it's almost guaranteed."

"And what about the mine?" Tabor asked. "What's the word from there?"

"Much of the same, I'm afraid, sir," Grant said.

"Then I suppose it's a good thing we heard that Lady Gunsmith was headed this way, eh?"

"Oh, yes sir," George Grant said, "very fortunate, indeed, sir."

"All right," Tabor said. "You can go, Grant. Just make sure she gets here tomorrow night."

"Yes, sir," Grant said, "I'll take care of it, personally."

As Grant headed for the door Tabor said, “One more thing.”

“Yes, sir?” Grant asked, turning.

“What’s the word on my wife?”

“Comfortably ensconced in your home in Denver, sir,” Grant said. “That’s the word I got.”

“Excellent!”

He went back to his book, ignoring Grant, and the man eventually turned and left.

***

After Grant left, Horace Tabor rose, walked to the sidebar and poured himself a snifter of very expensive brandy. He had wanted a glass while Grant was there, but had no desire to share it with the man, so he waited until he had gone. Now he carried it to his chair and sat back down. He took a sip, then set it aside on the table at his elbow and opened the book again.

Hopefully, with the presence of Lady Gunsmith in Leadville, conditions were going to improve.

Chapter Five

Roxy made the most of her luxurious free suite. She slept later than she usually did in that big bed, then enjoyed another long, lingering bath before getting dressed and coming downstairs for breakfast.

As she stopped in the doorway that led to the large dining room, a stiff man in a tuxedo came up to her and asked, “Is that gun really necessary, Miss?”

“Yes,” she said, “it is.”

“I’m afraid I can’t seat you—”

“Check with the front desk, friend” she said, cutting him off. “I’m Horace Tabor’s guest.”

“Oh, of course,” the man said, thawing out not an inch, “Miss Doyle, is it?”

“That’s right.”

“Follow me, please.”

She followed him across the crowded dining room to a table in the back of the room, exactly where she would have asked to be seated. This was one of the first lessons she learned from Clint Adams, the Gunsmith. Always sit so you could see the entire room, and no one can come up behind you.

He held her chair for her as she sat.

“Thank you.”

"Of course, Miss." The tuxedoed man was tall, with slick black hair parted down the center. He looked to be about forty, or so. And she noticed that he never once undressed her with his eyes.

"A waiter will be right with you," he said.

"Thank you."

As he crossed the room, stopping to speak to the guests along the way, a portly waiter in his fifties rushed over to her.

"What can I get you, Miss?"

"I'll start with coffee, then ham-and-eggs and some biscuits, please."

"Of course," the man said, "coming right up."

She was happy that the waiter was not a young man who would fawn over her. It was nice sometimes, but most of the time she just wanted to be treated like anybody else. But, of course, she wasn't just anybody else. She was Lady Gunsmith, and Clint Adams had also warned her that once she went down that road, there was no turning back.

The waiter came with her coffee, poured it for her, left the pot and then went back to the kitchen. She drank, ignoring the looks from other diners.

When the waiter returned, he put down a plate of ham-and-eggs in front of her. It looked like half a dozen eggs and a ham steak.

“Thank you,” she said.

“Is it enough?” he asked. “We have been told to see to your every need.”

“It’s fine,” she said. “Plenty. You did great.”

The waiter smiled happily, and while he backed away said, “Just wave if you need anything else.”

“I will, thanks.”

She was ravenous and applied herself to her plate, surprised that it actually was just enough food for her—along with some biscuits.

***

So far Horace Tabor had given her a free room in his Grand Hotel, and a free meal. She also had a free supper coming that night. She wondered what else was on the man’s mind? What this was all about. He had a beautiful wife, so it had to be more than just meeting another woman.

Didn’t it?

She finished her breakfast and left the dining room, still with many eyes following her. It was just something she had to put up with, unless she wanted to cut off all her red hair, put on forty pounds, and lose some teeth.

She preferred to just put up with the attention. She was certainly able to take care of herself if it got too . . . intense.

"I hope you enjoyed your breakfast," the tuxedoed man said, at the door.

"It was wonderful."

"And the service?"

"Great."

"I hope you'll tell Mr. Tabor that."

"I'm actually having supper with him tonight," she said. "What's your name?"

"Standish."

"And my waiter?"

"That was Thomas."

"Great," she said. "I'll see you boys again."

She walked across the lobby, unconcerned about whether or not he was watching her. Roxy Doyle was still a young woman, in her early twenties, but her experiences had aged her beyond her years. And that was going all the way back to when she was a child, and her foster father had raped her. She now felt able to handle men of all ages, gun or no gun, young or older. She wasn't intimidated at all by the thought of having supper with the richest man in Colorado. She was, however, curious about him, and his young, beautiful wife. So she was actually looking forward to going to Tabor's house that evening.

And she would also be happy to tell him how well his hotel staff had treated her during her stay.

She went up the stairs and returned to her room. What better place could there be to spend her time while waiting for supper with Horace Tabor? She could go out and walk for hours, and not find a more beautiful spot.

For the Grand Hotel was, indeed, grand.

Chapter Six

Roxy took another bath—it was going to be a long time before she had the opportunity to bathe in so leisurely a fashion—and then got dressed for dinner. She went to the closet and found a dress that fit her, tried it on, and then put it back. She dressed in her own clothes, the same trousers but a clean shirt from her saddlebags. She was willing to allow Tabor to feed her, but not to dress her. She was no man's plaything. She might have to make that clear to him.

She didn't know exactly what time to go downstairs to the lobby to wait for her buggy, but as she was about to leave, there was a knock at the door. When she opened it a crack to look out, she saw George Grant standing there.

"Ah, Miss Doyle," he said. "I've come to take you to your supper with Mr. Tabor."

She opened the door all the way and said, "I'm ready."

"Dressed like that?" he asked, looking surprised.

"These are my clothes, Mr. Grant."

"But the closet—"

"Is full of fine dresses," she said, "but I prefer my own clothes, thank you."

"And the gun?"

"The gun goes everywhere with me," she said. "I'm sure you know that."

"Well, yes, I suppose you're right," Grant said. "It's just that—well, I would hate for anything to happen to Mr. Tabor."

"I'm only going to have supper with him," Roxy reminded the man. "Not kill him."

"Well," Grant said, "that *is* a relief. Shall we go?"

"By all means."

She closed and locked her door, followed him down the stairs, across the lobby, out the front door and into a waiting buggy.

"You know where to go, Leon," he said to the driver.

"Yes, sir."

Roxy sat back to enjoy the ride.

***

Horace Tabor's house was a stately mansion, standing off by itself, although there were others in the area. None of them, however, could match his two story home that looked as if it had been lifted from a southern plantation. There were four white columns in front, and a porch that wrapped around.

The driver pulled the buggy to a stop in front. Grant hurriedly got out, then turned and extended a hand to

Roxy to help her. She could have gotten out on her own very well, but decided to take the man's offered hand.

"Thank you," she said.

They had not talked at all during the twenty-minute ride. In fact, Grant had pretty much stared straight ahead the whole way. On the other hand, the driver—a younger man—kept stealing glances over his shoulder at Roxy, who rewarded him with a smile each time.

"Come back in a few hours, Leon," Grant said. "The lady should be ready to return to the hotel by then."

"Yes, sir." He looked at Roxy. "Miss."

"See you later, Leon," she said.

She followed Grant up the tiled walkway to the front porch, and to the front door, where he knocked. The door was almost immediately opened by a black man wearing a white jacket.

"Good evening, Solomon," Grant said.

"Mr. Grant."

"This is Miss Doyle," Grant said. "Mr. Tabor's supper guest."

"Of course."

Grant looked at Roxy.

"Solomon will take you in," he said.

"You're not eating with us?" Roxy asked.

"No, no," George Grant told her, "it will just be you and Mr. Tabor."

"But . . . you sent the buggy away."

"It's a mild night," Grant said. "I prefer to walk."

"Will you be back?" she asked.

"No, Leon will return and drive you back to the hotel. Please, enjoy your meal."

He turned and walked back down the tiled walkway.

"Miss," Solomon said, "if you will follow me?"

Chapter Seven

Solomon led Roxy to a large dining room with a long, mahogany table, the top gleamed. It reflected the light from the crystal chandelier that hung above.

"Mr. Tabor will be with you in moments, Miss," Solomon said. "Would you like a drink while you wait?"

"No, thanks."

"May I take your gun?"

"No, you may not."

Solomon looked concerned.

"But Mr. Tabor does not like guns at the table," he told her.

"I'm afraid he'll have to put up with this one," she commented.

"I'm sorry, Miss, but—"

"It's all right, Solomon," a man said, as he entered the room. "Miss Doyle can keep her gun."

"As you wish, sir," Solomon said.

"Would you see how cook is coming along?" the man asked.

"Yes, sir."

The man turned to Roxy. He wore an expensive suit and smiled at her from behind his handlebar mustache.

"Miss Doyle, I am Horace Tabor."

"It's a pleasure to meet you Mr. Tabor," she said. "I've heard so much about you since I got to town."

"All of it good, I hope."

"Interesting."

"Well," Tabor said, "I've heard interesting things about you, too."

"Like what?"

"For one thing, I heard you were quite beautiful."

"And?"

"You were undersold," Tabor said. "You're the most beautiful woman I've ever seen."

"I thought that was your wife."

"Oh, Elizabeth is quite beautiful," Tabor agreed. "You'll have to meet her some time."

"Maybe before that," Roxy said, "I can find out why I'm here, and in your hotel."

"Why don't we sit down and eat," Tabor said, "and I'll tell you all about it."

At that moment, a middle-aged woman carrying a tray entered, followed by Solomon, who was also carrying a tray.

Tabor held a chair out for Roxy and she sat. He then circled the table and sat at the other end. That left them the length of the table away from each other.

"You may serve us," Tabor told Solomon.

"Yes, sir."

He and the cook put their trays down on a sideboard, and Solomon filled two bowls while the woman went back to the kitchen.

The first course was soup. Then the black houseman poured them each a glass of wine and withdrew.

"I hope you don't mind," Tabor said. "The wine, I mean."

"It's fine."

"Try the soup, then," Tabor said. "I think you'll like it."

She took a spoonful. It was chicken with wild rice.

"It's very good," she said. "So tell me, Mr. Tabor—"

"Please," he said, "call me Horace. May I call you Roxy?"

"Not yet," she said. "Let's stick with Miss Doyle for now."

He laughed shortly and said, "Very well, Miss Doyle."

"How did you know I was in Leadville, Horace?" she asked.

"I live here and in Denver," he said, "but I have eyes and ears in many places. You rode in here from a town called Buena Vista."

"That's right," she said. "It's about thirty miles away."

"Well," he said, "before you had gone ten miles, I heard you were on your way."

"How did you know I'd stop here?" she asked.

"I didn't know," he said. "I hoped, you see. After all, it's the largest town in this direction, unless you continue on to Denver."

"And how far is Denver?" she asked.

"Oh, a hundred miles or so," he said. "That's why I have a home in each place, for when I have to come here for business."

"Your Matchless Mine," she said.

"Exactly."

"And how did you know what hotel I was in?" she asked.

"Ah, I didn't," he said. "We checked every hotel in town. I must admit, the one we found you in was one of the last. Have you finished your soup?"

She'd eaten about half of it, but she said, "Yes, I have."

"Solomon!"

The black man came back in, collected their soup bowls, went to the sideboard and returned with a plate for each of them.

"Cook does amazing things with turkey," he said to Roxy.

"It's smells wonderful."

There were several slices of white turkey meat on her plate, and a healthy serving of mashed potatoes, covered with a light brown gravy. Also on the plate were some carrots. Solomon then placed a smaller plate next to her, which contained two rolls, and did the same for his boss.

"Thank you, Solly," Tabor said.

"Enjoy, sir," he said, with a bow, "Miss."

The black man left the room.

"I simply couldn't have you staying in a place like that," Tabor went on, "so I had your things moved. How is your suite, by the way?"

"It's wonderful."

"And have you been treated well by the staff?"

"Yes," she said. "The front desk, and the dining room staff have been very polite."

"Excellent! Eat up, then."

Tabor cut into his own turkey and chewed enthusiastically. Roxy took a smaller bite, but ended up eating with as much enthusiasm.

"Wow," she said, "this is tasty."

"I'm glad you like it," he said. "You know, I'm very impressed with you."

"Why is that?"

"Well, judging just by your reputation, I expected you to be—now don't be insulted—but a little rougher around the edges."

“I’m not insulted, at all. Because of my reputation, I’ve had to educate myself along the way.”

“And you’re so very young” he said. “I didn’t expect that, either.”

“I’m glad I’m not a disappointment to you,” she said.

“Oh hardly,” he said. “I just wish you had worn one of the dresses that was in your hotel room closet. Not that you’re not exquisite the way you’re dressed now, but, I mean . . . well, you understand.”

“And I hope you understand,” she said, “I’m simply more comfortable in my own clothes.”

“And with your gun.”

“Especially with my gun.”

He laughed shortly, almost like a bark.

“I understand perfectly,” he said. “Do you mind if we eat before it gets cold, and then continue talking after?”

“With this turkey?” she said, cutting into it again. “I don’t mind at all, Horace.”

They each turned their attention to the wonderfully prepared supper.

Chapter Eight

Once the plates had been cleared away, Solomon came back in with coffee and dessert. Roxy thought she smelled pie, but it turned out to be some sort of pastry.

"Cook is also a fine baker," Tabor told her.

"I agree," Roxy said, after a bite. "I'm afraid you're spoiling me, Horace, with this meal and your hotel. But it's time for you to tell me what you expect in return."

"Of course," he said. "Miss Doyle, I need your help."

Roxy laughed. She was in a fine mood after the food and wine, not to mention the pastry.

"I tell you what, Horace," she said. "You call me Roxy and tell me what I can do for you."

"I have need of your special talents."

"And what talent are you talking about?" she asked.

"Don't worry," he said, "I'm not going to try to avail myself of your beauty. As you yourself said, I have a beautiful wife."

"Then it must be my gun you want," she said. "I'm sorry, but it's not for sale. I don't hire out as a money gun."

"Well," Tabor said, "if I don't pay you, then you won't be selling your gun."

"Okay, let's not be hasty," she said. "I *do* need money."

"Then you'll have some, whether you help me or not," Tabor said. "Just for listening to my proposition."

"How much?"

"That's to be determined."

"I heard that when you met your wife you gave her five thousand dollars."

"Is that what you heard?" he asked, smiling. "Is that how much you want?"

"If I don't have to marry you for it."

"My wife wouldn't like that," Tabor said. "She likes being married to me."

"Well, make sure she knows I'm not interested in stealing you from her."

"It may not come to that," he said, "unless you go to Denver, or she comes here."

"We're getting off the subject," Roxy said.

"Ah, you mean, why have I lavished you with food and a hotel suite."

"Exactly."

Tabor pushed his empty dessert plate away.

"Have you finished eating?" he asked.

"I have."

"Then let's move," he said. "We'll go to my study and have a glass of brandy."

He stood, walked to her chair and pulled it out so she could rise.

***

Solomon opened the back door of the house in response to a knock. Cook watched as George Grant entered the kitchen.

“Coffee?” she asked.

“Thank you,” he said, “and maybe one of those pastries?”

“Sit,” she said, shortly.

Grant sat at the kitchen table. Solomon stood to one side as the cook served him.

“How’s it going?” Grant asked.

“They have finished supper,” Solomon said.

“Has Mr. Tabor gotten to the point?”

“Not yet.”

“So we don’t know if she’s going to agree.”

“Not yet.”

“Where are they?”

“In Mr. Tabor’s study,” Solomon said.

“Ah,” Grant said, “the good brandy. You know, he’s never offered me a glass of the good brandy.”

“But you have my pastry,” Cook said.

"Yes," Grant said, "that I have, and I'm enjoying it very much."

"Well, you better finish it and get out," Cook said, "before Mr. Tabor sees you."

"She's right," Solomon said.

"I know, I know," Grant said. "I was just . . . curious, is all."

He ate the last bite, washed it down with the last sip of coffee. Solomon held the door for him.

"See you, Solly," Grant said, and walked away.

Chapter Nine

In the study Tabor handed Roxy a glass of brandy, then poured one for himself.

"Please," he said, "sit."

There were two chairs in the center of the room. She took one, he the other. Between them was a small table. On it was the book he had been reading, but there was room for their glasses.

"Now," he said, settling into his chair, "you know about my Matchless Mine."

"Only the name," she said. "I'm not even sure what you're taking out of it."

"Lead," he said, "like the name of the town says."

"Ah."

"And as the owner of the largest mine in the area, I have to be careful."

"About what, exactly?"

"Thieves," he said, "con artists, even killers. The last time my payroll was brought in by a wagon, someone tried to steal it. Killed two of my men."

"But they didn't get the money?"

"No," he said, "they were interrupted by some of my men who went out to meet the wagon."

"That was lucky."

"Very lucky," Tabor said. "But that's just one thing. There's been accidents that aren't really accidents."

"Have you told the sheriff?"

"The sheriff is useless, here," Tabor said. "He arrests drunks and shoots stray dogs. He gets a nickel a piece."

"You have a lot of money," Roxy said. "What about Pinkertons?"

"I've had two here," he said.

"And?"

"They're both dead."

"How?"

"Accidents."

"That can't make the Pinkerton brothers happy," she said.

"They suggested I try another agency."

"And did you?"

"I was considering it . . . and then I heard you were in the area."

"I'm not a detective," she said.

"I've had detectives," he said. "And look what's happened."

"So what would you like me to do?"

"Make sure no more accidents happen," he said. "If men are afraid to work in my mine, how do I get my ore out? I'd have to shut it down."

"And what else?"

"Find out who's behind it," Tabor said, "who's trying to shut me down."

"You must have competitors."

"In other businesses, yes," he said. "I own hotels, restaurants, stocks . . . I have business rivals. But there's no mine around that can rival the Matchless."

"Why would someone be trying to shut you down," she asked, "if they're not going to profit from it?"

"I don't know!" For the first time, Tabor seemed to be losing his grip. "Look, I'll cover all your expenses while you're here, and I'll pay you five thousand dollars if you can put a stop to . . . to whatever's going on."

Roxy felt foolish for thinking that Horace Tabor might be after her as a woman. After all, he had a gorgeous wife. What the man wanted from her was help with his mine.

"Do you have any women working in the mine?" she asked.

"What? No, mining is not woman's work. All my miners are men. Why? Are you thinking of going . . . what's it called . . . undercover?"

"Maybe."

He brightened.

"Then you're considering helping me?"

"I'm considering it," she said, "if I think I could actually be helpful. And depending on how much time it would take."

"Ah, time," he said, "that's something I might be able to help you with."

"How do you mean?"

"I understand you've been looking for your father Gavin Doyle, the bounty hunter?"

"How would you know that?"

"Is it a secret?"

"No, not exactly."

"Like I told you, I have eyes and ears everywhere," he said. "Suppose while you're helping me, I help you."

"You mean—"

"—I'll find your father."

She sat forward in her chair.

"What makes you think you could do that?" she asked. "I've been searching for years."

"Then let me put it another way," Tabor said. "I'll try to get you some information that will help you find him."

She hesitated.

"Do you have any clue, at the moment, as to where he is?" Tabor asked.

"No," she said, "I've run down every rumor I've heard. I'm actually at a loss, right now. I'm . . . drifting."

"Then maybe we can help each other," Tabor said. "I'm drifting too, Roxy." He stood up, as if it would help him to make his point more strongly. "Let's see what we can do for each other."

Now she stood, left her brandy on the table.

"What do you say?" he asked.

"Horace," she said, "I say I'll give it a try."

He stuck his hand out.

"This is how I do business," he said.

They shook hands.

Chapter Ten

"Your buggy is outside," Tabor told Roxy.

"I'll need some of tomorrow to decide what I want to do, going forward," she said.

"Fine," Tabor said, "just let me know when you're ready to proceed."

"Will I come here and tell you?"

"Grant will be around," Tabor assured her. "Let him know."

"He's your right-hand man?"

Horace laughed.

"He's my gopher."

"But your mine has a foreman, right?"

"Yes," Tabor said, as they walked to the front door, "Gus Jensen."

"Okay, whatever I decide to do," she said, "I'll have to meet with him."

"You'll like Gus," Tabor said. "He's a good man."

"Fine," she said, at the door. "Thanks for supper, Horace. And for the hotel."

"Thank you for agreeing to help me, Roxy," he said. "I feel better, already."

"Glad to hear it."

As she stepped out, he said, "There's no chance you could get the Gunsmith to help, is there?"

"No," she said, "I don't even know where he is."

"I just thought I'd ask," Horace said, and closed the door.

***

Roxy rode the buggy back to her hotel in silence. The driver, Leon, kept stealing glances at her, but took the hint and stayed quiet.

In front of the hotel she stepped down from the buggy and said to the driver, "Thanks, Leon."

"My pleasure, Miss," the young man said. "Is there anything else I can do for you?"

Roxy studied the driver. He was a handsome youngster, perhaps a year or two younger than she was. She wasn't tired, so figured she needed something else to do before she could finally turn in. She wanted to think about Horace Tabor's offer, but first she needed something to distract her.

"Yes, there is, Leon," she said. "Why don't you park that buggy somewhere, and then come up to my room. I may have something for you to do."

"Yes, Ma'am!" he said.

She realized he understood what she meant, which was good. He was young, and not quite naïve.

She went inside, walked across the lobby and up to her room to await the young man.

***

When the knock came at the door, she answered it holding her gun, even though she was sure it was Leon.

"Oh," he said, surprised to see the gun.

"Come on in, Leon," she said. "Sorry about the gun Can't be too careful, you know."

"Sure," he said, "I know."

She put the gun back in the holster hanging on the bedpost and turned to face him.

"Do you know why I asked you to come up here?" she asked him.

"Um," he said, "I ain't sure, but I, uh, hoped . . ."

"I thought you needed a bath," she said.

"Huh?"

"Would you like to take a bath with me?" she asked. "I find a hot bath very soothing, don't you?"

"Oh, sure . . ."

"Let's go in there," she said, pointing.

"Okay."

He went ahead of her, into a room with a large bathtub, which surprised him.

"Right here in your room?"

"That's one of the reasons they call it the Grand Hotel," she told him.

She set the tub to fill with hot water, which also surprised him, and then said, "Why don't you get undressed?"

"You, uh, you mean . . ."

"Naked," she said. "I mean naked."

"Are, you, uh, gonna get naked, too?" he asked.

"That's the only way to take a bath, isn't it?" she asked, starting to unbutton her shirt.

"Oh, uh, yeah."

He started unbuttoning his own shirt, unsure where to look. When she was naked to the waist, though, he couldn't look anywhere else.

He staggered, trying to get his boots off, and then his trousers, while still watching her undress. The more and more flesh she exposed, the wider his eyes got.

Roxy had learned a long time ago that sex was a tool. After she was abused by her step father and step brother, she learned how to use sex to control them. When she left home, she learned how to use it to get what she wanted from men. Sometimes she used it for business, and other times—like now—she used it purely for pleasure. And she learned never to be ashamed of it.

When they were both naked, she approached him and took his rather large penis in her hand. Immediately, it began to swell even more. When he was good and hard, she tightened her hand around it and tugged, leading him to the bathtub.

"Let's climb in, Leon," she said, "and get each other nice and clean."

"Yes, Ma'am!"

Chapter Eleven

They washed each other good—every orifice—and she knew the young man was fighting to keep from squirting right there and then.

But once they were nice and clean she told him, “Sit up here, on the edge.”

He sat on the edge of the tub, his legs still in the water, but his cock bobbing up above. She got to her knees in front of him, stroked his cock and then took it into her mouth. Almost immediately, he exploded. When she finished draining him of every drop, she released him from her hot mouth.

“Jeez, I’m sorry,” he said, “I didn’t mean—”

“Oh, relax, Leon,” she said. “You don’t have any place else to be, do you?”

“No, Ma’am.”

“Well then we have plenty of time. Let’s dry off and move to the bed.”

“Yes, Ma’am!”

***

When they got to the bed, she kissed him, and he returned the kiss with enthusiasm. Lying on the bed together, she allowed him to explore her body all he wanted. He wasn't inexperienced. But neither was he expert. When he bit her nipples she enjoyed it, but when he put his hand down between her legs roughly, she had to guide him.

"Easy, Leon," she said, "go easy. Just stroke it. There you go, that's it, mmmm, that's good . . ."

By then his cock was good and hard again, so she flipped him on his back, mounted him and took it inside of her. She started to ride him, hoping he wouldn't finish too soon, again. She just needed him to stay hard long enough for her to get what she wanted and thankfully, since he had already ejaculated once, he managed to do just that.

He obviously had no knowledge of oral sex, though, and she decided she didn't have the time or patience to teach him. So she rode him to her climax, let him finish, as well, then got off and laid down beside him.

"Was that all right for you, Leon?" she asked.

"That was . . . oh, yes, Ma'am. Was it okay . . . I mean, for you?"

"It was fine," she said. "I got just what I needed. Now, you can get dressed and leave."

"Huh? I thought, well, maybe we could—"

"I need to get some sleep, and I can't do that with anyone else in the bed. You understand, don't you?"

"Oh, uh, sure." He got off the bed, retrieved his clothes and put them on. "Should I come back—I mean, tomorrow—"

He had a puppy dog look on his face which, at that moment, she found annoying.

"I don't think I'll need a ride tomorrow, Leon," she said, meaning it in two ways.

"Okay, well then, uh, good-night . . . I guess." He inched toward the door, as if he thought she might stop him before he got there.

"Good-night, Leon," she said, "and thanks."

When he left she got up, made sure the door was locked, then went back to bed. She felt very relaxed, both from the bath and from Leon. She touched the gun on the bedpost for a moment, then fell asleep . . .

***

When she woke in the morning, she stretched and thought about the night before. Not the sex with Leon. That had been unremarkable, and just a way to scratch an itch. With more practice the young man might become more adept, but some other girl was going to have to benefit from that.

No, what she thought about was the time she spent with Horace Tabor. That had been much more interesting. And the meal had been one of the best she'd had in a long time.

While she dressed she decided to use Tabor, both for his money, and for whatever information he could get her regarding where her father might be. She had just pulled on her boots when there was a knock at her door. She grabbed the gun from her gunbelt, went to the door and opened it a crack, expecting to see either Leon, or George Grant.

Instead, she saw a woman.

Not just any woman, though, a beautiful woman dressed very expensively. She had short dark hair, and glittering earrings with purple stones that matched her dress. Roxy knew who she was right away.

"Are you Roxy Doyle?" the woman asked.

"That's right." Roxy swung the door wide open. Horace Tabor's wife did not look surprised by the gun.

"I'm Elizabeth Tabor."

"Baby Doe," Roxy said, before she could stop herself.

"I hate that name," she said, "perhaps as much as you hate being called Lady Gunsmith, I think?"

"I understand, Mrs. Tabor."

"You don't look surprised."

"Somehow, I'm not," Roxy said. "I mean, when I saw you standing in the hall, you're so beautiful I just assumed you were Elizabeth Tabor."

"And I had heard how beautiful you were," Baby Doe said, "but you're breathtaking."

"Mrs. Tabor—"

"And now that we've gotten the compliments out of the way," Baby Doe said, cutting Roxy off, "why don't you tell me what the hell you were doing with my husband at our house, last night?"

Chapter Twelve

They decided to have the conversation someplace other than the hall. Roxy suggested inside the suite, but Baby Doe countered with the hotel dining room.

"I've come all the way from Denver, and I'm hungry."

"Well," Roxy said, "I'm ready for breakfast, myself."

They went downstairs, where the staff made a fuss about both of them.

The desk clerk came rushing out from behind the desk.

"Is there anything I can do for you ladies?"

"Oh, go back to work, Charles," Baby Doe said. "We're fine. We're just going to have something to eat."

"Together?"

"And why not?"

Charles put his hands up, as if to ward off a blow from his boss's wife, and said, "No reason, Mrs. Tabor, no reason at all."

When they got to the doorway of the dining room the maître d' said, "Ladies. May I show you to a table?"

"How else would we eat, Samuel?" Baby Doe demanded.

"Of course. You're usual table, Mrs. Tabor."

Baby Doe turned to Roxy.

"It's in the center of the room," she said. "Is that a problem for you?"

"Yes," Roxy said, "a big one."

"A back table, Ma'am?" Samuel asked Roxy.

"Is that a problem for you?" Roxy asked Baby Doe.

"Lead the way, Samuel."

"Of course, Madam."

He showed them to the same table Roxy had used before. All the other diners in the room looked up from their meals, or turned their heads, to watch the two beautiful women walk across the floor. Roxy figured Baby Doe was about five or six years older than her, almost thirty.

"I'll send a waiter over—" Samuel started.

"Oh, Samuel, just take our order!" Baby Doe snapped.

"Yes, Madam."

"A soft boiled egg for me, and a biscuit," Baby Doe said. "And a slice of melon."

"Ham-and eggs for me," Roxy said. "And coffee."

"Tea, for me," Baby Doe said.

"Of course."

As Samuel walked away, Baby Doe set her purse on the floor and looked across the table at Roxy.

"You were at my house last night," she said. "My Leadville house."

"Yes."

"Why?"

"Your husband invited me to supper."

"And you accepted?"

"I did."

"Had you ever met him before?"

"Never met him," Roxy said, "never saw him, never even heard of him."

"Then why did you accept?"

Roxy spread her arms, palms up, and said, "He made a convincing argument."

"I thought you said you didn't meet him?"

"It was a man named George Grant who made the case," Roxy explained.

"Ah, Horace's gopher here in Leadville."

"Not in Denver?"

"No," Baby Doe said, "there he has one named Hector."

"Ah."

A waiter came with their coffee and tea, and a basket of hot biscuits, with butter on the side.

"Thank you," Baby Doe said.

The waiter withdrew.

"So what did Horace want?" Baby Doe asked. "Did he give you any money?"

"I heard that story," Roxy said, buttering a biscuit. "Did he really give you five thousand dollars when you met?"

"He did," Baby Doe said, smiling at the memory. "He was also trying to make a good argument, then."

"That's a pretty good one."

"Did my husband make a case like that with you?" Mrs. Tabor asked.

"No." Roxy bit into her biscuit. "He's married to you, why would he be interested in me?"

"Suppose you answer your own question?" Baby Doe suggested.

The waiter came back, set their plates down in front of them, and left.

"You don't watch your figure, do you?" Elizabeth Doe asked.

"Not really."

"Of course not," she said. "You don't have to." She cut into her melon. "You're young."

"Just because you're older than I am," Roxy said, "doesn't make you old."

"Nevertheless," Baby Doe said, "I have to watch mine. If I eat the wrong thing on one day, I'm five pounds heavier the next."

Roxy put some ham-and-eggs into her mouth.

"Don't worry about what I weigh," she said.

Baby Doe stared across the table at her.

"Are you *trying* to make me hate you?"

"Your husband must be twenty years older than you."

"Twenty-five."

"It doesn't seem to me he's watching his figure for you," Roxy said. "I watched him eat, last night."

"Men don't have to do that," Baby Doe said. "Only women."

"That's not fair."

"It's not fair, at all," Mrs. Tabor said, grabbing a biscuit. "So?"

"Your husband wants to hire me, Mrs. Tabor," Roxy said.

"Hire you?" She lowered the biscuit without biting into it. "For what?"

"I really think you should ask him that, don't you?"

Chapter Thirteen

Roxy was surprised Baby Doe didn't push for a more definite answer. Instead, the women talked about other things over breakfast. By the end of the meal anyone watching might have thought they were friends.

Over a final cup of coffee and tea, Baby Doe Tabor said, "You know something, Roxy Doyle?"

"What?"

"I like you."

"I was told you would hate me on sight," Roxy said.

"And who told you that?" Baby Doe demanded.

"Several people."

"Was Grant one?"

"I wouldn't want to get him into trouble."

"And Horace?"

"No," Roxy said, "your husband only said good things about you."

"That's because he wasn't trying to get your clothes off," Baby Doe said.

"No," Roxy said, "and if he was trying, he wouldn't have succeeded."

"Speaking of clothes," Baby Doe said, "I'm going shopping. Would you like to come? There are a couple of good stores here in Leadville."

“I don’t think I wear the same kind of clothes you do,” Roxy said.

“You could,” Baby Doe said. “With your figure, you could wear anything.”

“I’m afraid I’m not here to shop,” Roxy said. “And besides, I don’t have any money.”

“Not any?”

“A few dollars,” Roxy said. “Luckily, I don’t have to pay for my room, or my food, as long as I eat here.”

“You’re very frank,” Baby Doe said. “Now I like you even more.” They stood and walked out of the dining room under many watchful eyes. The maître d’ rushed after them.

“Was everything satisfactory?”

“Yes, very satisfactory,” Baby Doe said. “Your job is safe.”

“Thank you, Madam.”

Baby Doe and Roxy went into the lobby.

“I have a suite here,” Baby Doe told her, “and I’ll be here for a few days.”

“You’re not staying with your husband?”

“He’s here conducting business,” she said. “I don’t like to get in his way. Besides, the shopping I want to do is near here.”

“I see.”

Baby Doe stood back a step and regarded Roxy from head to toe.

"My God," she said, "I wish you'd let me dress you. You're beautiful now, but when I'm through with you, you'll be stunning."

"I don't think I have time for that," Roxy said, then added, "Yet."

"Well," Baby Doe said, "I'll be here if you change your mind. On the floor above yours."

"I'll remember."

"And whatever my husband wants you to do," she said, "make sure he pays you very well to do it."

"We have an agreement," Roxy assured her.

"My husband's a businessman," Baby Doe said. "You make sure he sticks to that arrangement, no matter what you have to do. Do you understand?"

Roxy considered that a warning.

"I believe I do," she said.

***

Solomon let George Grant in the front door and took him to the dining room, where Horace Tabor was enjoying a lavish breakfast.

"Ah, Grant," Tabor said. "I'd invite you to eat, but I usually enjoy eating alone."

"I understand."

"What brings you here so early?"

"Your wife, sir."

"What about her?"

"She's here."

"Here? Here . . . where, exactly?"

"In Leadville, sir," Grant said. "She has a suite at the Grand."

"She must be here to shop, then," Tabor said.

"That's possible," Grant said, "but . . ."

"But what?"

Grant hesitated.

"Come on, spit it out, man!"

"She's having breakfast with Roxy Doyle this morning," Grant said. "In the hotel dining room."

"What?" Tabor stood up abruptly. "Why wasn't I told about this sooner?"

"I only heard about it myself, sir, just a short while ago."

"You should have heard about it as soon as she left Denver!" Tabor said.

"Yes, well," Grant said, "to get here this early, sir, she must have left Denver while it was still dark."

"She snuck out of the city, you mean."

"Yes, sir."

Tabor took only a moment to make up his mind.

"Get out, George!"

"What do you want me to do—"

"I just told you what I want you to do," Tabor said. "Get . . . out!"

"Yessir."

Grant hurried from the dining room. Tabor and Solomon heard the front door open and close.

"Have my carriage brought around, Solly."

"Yes, sir."

Tabor regarded his half-finished breakfast, then turned and stalked out of the room.

Chapter Fourteen

Before making her final decision, Roxy decided she needed to talk to someone not named Tabor. That meant locating Horace's man, George Grant. So when Elizabeth Tabor went up to her suite after their afternoon of shopping, Roxy remained in the lobby, to see how long it took Grant to arrive.

It didn't take long.

Twenty minutes later Grant walked in the front door. He spotted Roxy's red hair as soon as he entered. She stood up and approached him.

"Hello, Mr. Grant."

"Miss Doyle."

"Are you looking for me?"

"Actually, no, I was just, uh . . ."

"Looking for Mrs. Tabor?"

Grant hesitated then said, "Well, yes."

"She's up in her room," Roxy said. "We had a nice breakfast together."

"Really?"

"I like her," Roxy said.

"That's, uh, good."

"How about we have a cup of coffee, George?" Roxy asked.

"Mr. Tabor wanted me to go up and check on Baby—on Mrs. Tabor," Grant said.

"You can do that later," Roxy said. "I want to talk to you."

"Oh? About what?"

"Your boss," Roxy said. "Come on, I'll buy."

***

Moments later they were in the bar of the Grand Hotel, each with a drink in front of them, instead of coffee.

"What's on your mind, Miss Doyle?"

"What's your job, Mr. Grant?"

"I am Mr. Tabor's assistant," Grant said. "His right-hand man, if you will."

"His gopher?"

Grant frowned and shook his head.

"That's not a term I would use."

"Funny," she said, "that's the term he used. It's the term his wife used, too."

Grant didn't respond.

"Do you know a man named Hector?"

"He's . . . Mr. Tabor's assistant in Denver."

"He's the Denver gopher," she said. "And you're the Leadville gopher."

He picked up his drink, a glass of brandy, and sipped it.

"Does he share his good brandy with you?" Roxy asked.

Grant set his glass down.

"What is it you want to know?"

"Your boss wants me to clean up some kind of mess at his mine," Roxy said.

"So?"

"So is that what he really wants?" Roxy asked. "Or am I being set up for something?"

Grant picked up his drink, sipped it, and put it down.

"There *is* a problem at the mine," he said.

"And some Pinkertons were killed?"

"They . . . went missing."

"But presumed dead."

"Yes."

"So he really needs help."

"He does. He was thinking about hiring someone . . . good with a gun."

"But?"

"He couldn't figure out who," Grant said. "He thought about other detectives—James Hume, Heck Thomas, Talbot Roper—but could never make up his mind. And then . . ."

"And then he heard I was in the area."

Grant nodded.

"He was even thinking about trying to find Clint Adams," Grant said, "you know, the Gunsmith?"

"I know who the Gunsmith is."

"Yes, of course you do," Grant said. "So he's made his offer to you?"

"He has."

"What are you going to do?"

"Well," Roxy said, "I can use the money, but I feel like I'm selling my gun."

"Don't you hire your gun out?" Grant asked. "Isn't that what you do?"

"No," she said, "that's the problem. It's not what I do."

"Your reputation—"

"Reputations aren't real," she said, cutting him off.

"So you've never killed anybody?"

"Nobody who didn't deserve it," she replied, "and left me no other choice."

"So this could be the same thing."

"Yeah, it could be."

They both picked up their drinks—Roxy had a beer—and sipped.

"What did you tell Mrs. Tabor?"

"Everything."

He raised his eyebrows.

"Mr. Tabor might not like that."

"I couldn't have her think I was sleeping with him."

"No," Grant said, "I guess you couldn't."

She studied him for a moment, then said, "Tell me something, George."

"Yes?"

"You're not involved in what's going on up at the mine, are you?"

He took a moment before speaking.

"You're already on the job, aren't you?" he asked.

Chapter Fifteen

Roxy didn't know what she had done to Horace Tabor and George Grant's working relationship, but she had gotten what she wanted. Or rather, what she needed. She had confirmation that Tabor's Matchless Mine really was having trouble, so her next step was to ride up there. Before leaving George Grant to finish his brandy, she got him to give her directions and some expense money.

"It's only a few hours ride," he told her, "but some of it is pretty treacherous. You'll need a good horse."

"Not the one I rode in on, then," she said. "I'm going to need to buy a new one."

"Mr. Tabor thought you might," Grant said, "so he asked me to give you this." He took some money from his pocket and handed it to her. "Expenses."

As they left the hotel Roxy asked Grant, "So, were you on your way to see me at the hotel?"

"I was to check on Mrs. Tabor," he said, "but I was carrying that money for you, just in case."

"Well, I'm glad you were," she said. "You can tell your boss I'm going to outfit myself today and ride up to the mine tomorrow."

“You’ll want to see Gus Jensen,” Grant said, “He’s the foreman. You and Gus will have to decide how you’re going to handle the situation.”

“He knows I’m coming?” she asked.

“I sent him a message.”

“Saying what?”

“Just that you’d be riding up, and he’s to give you every bit of cooperation he can.”

“And nobody else up there knows about me?” she asked.

“Not unless Gus told someone.”

He left Roxy and crossed back to the hotel side of the street. She waited to watch him enter before she turned and left.

***

Since it was only a few hours ride to the mine she decided to spend most of the money Grant had given her on a good horse. She wouldn’t need much in the way of supplies. She took her time studying the mounts and ended up with a sure footed little paint about four years old. She paid cash, and threw in the horse she rode in on, an eight-year-old steeldust who still had some mileage left on him.

She arranged for the hostler to saddle the horse for her come morning, and walk it over to the hotel.

"Will you need anythin' else, Miss?" the man asked. "Supplies?"

"I'll have what I need," she assured him, "just bring the horse to the hotel at seven."

"Yes, Miss."

She left the livery and stopped into a general store she had passed along the way. All she bought was some coffee, and beef jerky. She had everything else she needed.

She went back to her hotel, carrying her purchases in her left hand.

***

When Grant appeared at Baby Doe's door she said, "Oh, come in, George."

She was wearing an expensive dressing gown, and her hair was down. She was quite beautiful, but Grant couldn't see how she would get along with someone like Roxy Doyle, who might have been even more lovely.

"Close the door!" she said, impatiently.

George Grant had known very few beautiful women. Judging by Baby Doe Tabor, they were rude and bad tempered. But now that he had met Roxy Doyle, he saw they were not all that way.

“Have you told Horace I’m in town?” she asked.

“Yes, Ma’am.”

“Was he mad?”

“Yes.”

“So he’ll be coming here to see me.”

“I expect he will,” Grant said.

“Good,” she said, rifling through one of the three bags she had brought with her and put on the bed. “I’ve been wanting to talk to him.” She turned to face Grant. “And did you tell him I had breakfast with Roxy?”

“I did.”

“You’re doing your job very well, George.” She returned to her bag.

“Thank you, Madam,” he said. “I also just had a drink with Miss Doyle.”

“Oh?” she turned to face him again. “What was that about?”

“She wanted to make sure there really was trouble at the mine, and she wasn’t being . . . used, somehow.”

“If she’s paid, she’s paid to be used, right?” Baby Doe asked.

“I don’t know that she sees it that way, Madam.”

“No, she probably has her own way of seeing things, doesn’t she, George?”

"I think so."

She laughed.

"Then that makes two of us," she said. "I like her very much. Does that surprise you?"

"Yes, Madam."

"Why?"

Grant hesitated, then asked, "May I be frank?"

"I wish you would." Now she completely ignored her bag and gave him her undivided attention.

"She's very beautiful."

She waited for more, and when it didn't come, she asked, "And you thought I'd dislike her for that reason?"

"Yes, Miss."

She turned back to her bag and tossed it over her shoulder, "That'll be all, George."

"Yes, Ma'am," he said, and left.

She turned her head and said, to the door, "Gopher!"

Chapter Sixteen

Roxy went to her room after a quick meal and stuffed the coffee and beef jerky into her saddlebags, then set them aside. All that was left was to get some sleep and then get up to the Matchless Mine early and see what she could find out. She knew Baby Doe had a suite—probably bigger than hers—on the floor above her, but she had no reason to see the woman again. She was working for Horace Tabor, not Baby Doe Tabor.

She was just settling onto the bed, boots off, shirt unbuttoned, pants still on, when there was a knock at the door. She took her gun from the holster and carried it to the door.

"Who is it?"

"Elizabeth Tabor," a woman's voice said. Then: "Baby Doe?"

Roxy opened the door, peered out, saw Baby Doe standing there in her dressing gown, and opened it all the way.

"You better come in before somebody sees you out there," she said.

"What, you mean in this? Don't worry—oh, all right." Baby Doe stepped inside and Roxy closed the door.

Once inside Roxy walked to the bedpost to holster her gun, then began to button her shirt.

"You don't have to do that," Baby Doe said. "It's your room. Stay comfortable. Besides, I won't be here long."

Roxy stopped buttoning the shirt, but folded her arms across her breasts.

"What's on your mind, Elizabeth?"

"Are you going up to the mine soon?"

"Tomorrow."

"That *is* soon," Elizabeth said. "I want to go with you."

"I don't think so."

"I think I should."

"Why?"

"Because Horace doesn't tell me anything," she said. "And I want to know what's going on."

"Look," Roxy said, "I won't know 'til I get there how I'm going to handle this. I have to talk to the foreman. I may end up giving him a false name. But if you're with me, everybody knows you. They'll know I'm working for you or your husband." She unfolded her arms. "I have to go alone."

After a moment Elizabeth said, "All right, I get that. But would you let me know what you find out? I don't like living in the dark."

Roxy thought a moment, then said, “Yes, all right.”

“And I won’t necessarily tell Horace anything you tell me,” the woman said. “You can trust me.”

“I will,” Roxy said.

Elizabeth nodded, and moved to the door, then turned.

“Thank you, Roxy.”

“You’re welcome, Elizabeth.”

Baby Doe Tabor went out the door.

Roxy sat on the bed, wondering what was really going on between Horace and Elizabeth Tabor, and if it had anything to do with the trouble at the mine.

She’d find out more tomorrow.

***

When Baby Doe reentered her room on the third floor, Horace Tabor stood up from the bed.

“Well?”

“She’ll talk to me,” she said. “Keep me informed.”

“Good, that’s good.”

“You know,” she said, “if you would keep *me* informed, I wouldn’t have had to come all this way from Denver.”

He sat on the bed with his back against the bedpost, crossed his legs, and asked. “What would you like to know, my dear?”

"I needed to know why you sent for a beautiful red-haired gunfighter," she said. "for her gun, or for something else?"

"Why would I ever need another woman when I have you, my dear?" Horace asked. "Of course, I need her gun, and I also need her reputation."

"And do you have those things?"

"I believe so," Tabor said. "As usual, I talked money, and somebody listened."

"Oh, you think she wants your money."

"Isn't that what everybody wants from me?"

"Is that why you're having trouble at the mine?"

Tabor didn't look happy with the question. He brought his feet around to the floor and stood up.

"The mine is my business, Elizabeth," he said, his tone a warning one.

"I just want to be helpful, dear," she said. "Did you marry me just for my looks?"

"No," Tabor said, "no, of course not." He walked to her and took her hand. "I, of all people, know there is more to you than just your beauty."

"Then don't keep me in the dark, anymore," she said. "Please."

"Very well," he said, and embraced her.

"And now" she said, "since you're here, why don't we go to bed?"

"I would like nothing more," he assured her.

***

In her room Roxy got into bed, reached up to touch her gun before turning out the lamp. She felt she had accomplished something that day with her conversations with Grant and Baby Doe. It seemed like Horace Tabor really did need her help up at his Matchless Mine. But that didn't mean the man didn't have some other plans, as well. Roxy was just going to have to stay alert. Hopefully she'd solve the mine problem, and come out of it with enough money to continue her search for her father . . . and with information about where to start.

But she needed one more good-night's sleep in this plush bed before she got started.

Chapter Seventeen

In the morning Roxy had a quick breakfast, and then left the hotel with her saddlebags. She didn't bother checking out since she wasn't paying for the room, and it would probably be held for her until she got back.

Out front stood the hostler with her new horse, all saddled and ready to go.

"Thank you," she said to him.

"My pleasure, Miss," he said, holding the horse's head while she mounted up. "This sure-footed little guy will get you where you're goin'—wherever that is."

She smiled at him, nodded and gave the horse her heels to spur him on.

"His name is Little Joe!" he called after her.

***

She rode for a couple of hours, then reined in the horse for a short rest.

She dismounted and allowed him to graze.

"Little Joe," she said. "I really didn't need to know your name. I prefer my horses to be expendable. Knowing your name gives you a kind of personality. I don't need a horse with a personality I just need a horse with four legs."

She realized she was talking to the animal, which gave him even more of what she didn't need. Also, she didn't need to talk since her breathing was coming with some difficulty. Leadville was at an elevation of ten thousand feet, and the mine was above that. The hostler had assured her the horse would be able to handle the climb, "but you oughtta go slow, until you get used to it."

She took a drink of water, then remounted and started back up the hill in front of her, wondering how far up the mountain the mine actually was?

***

By the time Roxy reached the mine—she had no idea how high up she was, but it was high—she could hardly catch her breath. She decided it wouldn't do to arrive gasping for air, so she decided to stop and wait until her breathing had returned to something resembling normal.

Once she felt better, she remounted and rode into the mining camp. Several of the men stopped what they were doing to watch her ride by. Others gathered in front of the building that must have been the mining office, waiting for her to stop and dismount.

"Can we help ya, little lady?" one man asked.

They were all dressed in clothes, filthy from the mines. They were also sweaty and covered with dirt and dust. But they were smiling at her, as if they were so happy to see something other than the inside of a mountain.

"I'm looking for Gus Jensen."

"Why Gus?" he asked. "Won't one of us do?"

Before she could answer, the door to the office opened, and a tall, handsome man with broad shoulders walked out. He was dressed as the others, but clean.

"All right, that's enough," he said, "I don't think this young lady is gonna be interested in any of you sweaty bums. Get back to work."

They started to move away, but the spokesman called to Roxy, "When you get bored with Gus, come and see me."

"Move, Dawkins!" Gus snapped.

As all the men headed back to work, Gus Jensen turned and looked at Roxy.

"What's a beautiful girl like you doin' up here? Are you lost?" he asked.

"I'm looking for Gus Jensen," she said. "I'm going to assume that's you."

"It's me, all right. And you are . . ."

"Roxy Doyle," she said. "Mr. Tabor sent me up here."

That struck a chord with him.

"We better talk inside," he said. "After you."

She tied her horse off and then entered the office. He came in behind her and shut the door.

"How about a drink?" he asked. "You probably need it after that long ride uphill."

"That'd be great."

"Whiskey or water?" he asked.

"Both, please."

He poured some whiskey into a glass and then topped it off with water. For himself he poured two fingers of whiskey.

"I can also offer you some water to wash with, if you like," he said.

She drank half the glass down and said, "That sounds wonderful."

He went into another room and she watched the muscles in his arms as he pumped some water for her into a sink.

"There you go," he said. "All the comforts of home. I'm sorry, but for other comforts you'd still need to use the privy out back."

"This will be fine for now."

She finished her drink, set the glass down, then went into the smaller room, rolled up her sleeves and washed her hands, arms and face. With him watching, that was as far as she was willing to go, at the moment.

She came back out, drying herself with a towel. She looked at his square-jawed, handsome face, and the twinkle in his blue eyes as he stared back. He looked to be in his late thirties.

"So you're Lady Gunsmith," he said, then.

"That's me."

"And Horace seemed to think you can solve the problems we've been having up here when two different Pinkertons couldn't?"

"He must think I have something to offer that they didn't," she said, setting the towel aside. "Can I have some more water, please?"

"Just water?"

"Yes."

He filled her glass and handed it to her. She drank it down, clearing her throat of trail dust, and set it aside.

"Now," she said, "why don't you tell me exactly what's been happening?"

Chapter Eighteen

She listened while he described a litany of accidents, robberies and even murders that had been happening over the past few months.

"Somebody's obviously trying to sabotage your whole operation," she said.

"Obviously."

"And neither you nor Mr. Tabor have any idea who it might be?" she asked.

"I haven't a clue," he said, "but you'd think Horace would have some idea. I mean, a rich man like him, he's probably pissed off a lot of people. You'd think more than one would be capable of somethin' like this."

"And what about Mrs. Tabor?"

"What about her?"

"Do you know her?"

"Well, I've met her once or twice, but she doesn't have anythin' to do with the day-to-day operations up here."

"She's a beautiful woman," Roxy said.

"She is that," he agreed.

"And you're a good-looking man."

"I'm flattered," he said, "but I hope you're not insinuating that there's anythin' between her and me. I sure as hell don't know her that well."

"Okay," Roxy said, "I was just checking."

"So what do you intend to do?" Jensen asked.

"Well," she said, "I'm going to have to stay a while, have a look around, and hopefully be here when the next 'accident' occurs."

"Stay up here?" he asked. "Where. All we have is the one bunkhouse. Even I have to sleep with the men."

"I could sleep a little bit away from the main part of camp," she said.

He looked around.

"I suppose I could set up a bed for you in here," he said.

"Horace said he expected you and me to come up with a plan," she explained.

"What should we tell the men?" he asked. "I could say that Horace hired you to be my assistant."

"An assistant with a gun?"

"You could take it off," he suggested.

"I'm afraid that would be a deal breaker," she said. "I'd rather just ride back to Leadville and forget the whole thing."

"Okay, okay," he said, "I forgot for a moment who I was talkin' to. Of course you wouldn't take your gun off."

"Why do we need to lie?" she asked.

"Well, the Pinkertons were here as miners," he said. "Nobody knew who they really were."

"Somebody did," she said.

"Right."

"Besides," she said, "if we let it be known why I'm really here, maybe that would be enough to discourage whoever's behind all this."

"You think this would all stop just because you're here?"

She shrugged.

"Who knows? It can't hurt to let them know I'm around."

"What if they try to kill you?"

"They'll find it a lot harder than killing two Pinkertons. By the way how did they die?"

"Those mining accidents I told you weren't accidents?" Jensen said. "That's how they both died, in cave-ins. We had to dig 'em out after."

"Do you think the sabotage and killings are being done by somebody inside your camp?"

"No."

"How can you be so sure?"

"Because I personally hired all these men. I vouch for them. They're miners, not killers."

"Enough money can turn anybody into a killer," she said.

"We're payin' them plenty."

"Okay," she said, looking around the interior of the small office. There was a table that was slightly slanted, and some chairs. On the table were some papers.

"I don't think you need to put in any kind of bed," she said. "I'm pretty sure I can sleep on my bedroll. Is there someplace we can put my horse?"

"There's a leanto out back. We have a couple of horses in there, now."

"That'll do. Feed?"

"We've got enough," he said. "I'll have somebody put your horse back there."

"Let me get my saddlebags and bedroll."

They went out together, and while Jensen went to find somebody to take care of her horse, she got her saddlebags, bedroll, and rifle and took them inside. She set everything aside and went to the slanted table to look at the papers. They appeared to be like maps of the inside of the different mine shafts.

"That's a drafting table," a man's voice said. "That's why it's slanted like that."

She turned and saw a short, stocky man in his forties standing in the doorway. He closed the door and crossed the room to her.

"These are plans for shafts one and two," he said. "You ever been in a mining camp before?"

"No, I haven't."

He put his hand out.

"I'm Stan Riley, the engineer on this operation."

"Mr. Riley," she said. "Roxy Doyle."

"I figured."

"Why's that?"

"I've heard of you," he said. "And there can't be that many women around who look like you."

"I suppose I should take that as a compliment."

"I meant with the gun and all."

"Oh."

At that point Jensen came back in, saying, "Okay, your horse is—oh, you met Stan."

"Yes," she said, "Mr. Riley was just telling me how he knew who I was."

"Well," Jensen said, closing the door, "then that cat's out of the bag. No use discussing it further."

"Sorry," Riley said, "but if you want this woman to go unnoticed—"

"I know," Jensen said, "we can forget it. Lady Gunsmith is very noticeable."

"Well," Roxy said, "let's see if it does any good."

Chapter Nineteen

Roxy knew the difference between her presence and that of the Pinkertons. The Pinks were trying to pass themselves off as miners. Roxy was simply going to be Roxy Doyle, Lady Gunsmith, there because she was trying to figure out who was sabotaging the Matchless Mine and costing Horace Tabor a lot of money. If somebody wanted to stop her, let them try.

She was putting a target on her back because, one, she wasn't a detective. And two, in her young life she had become used to it. Clint Adams, the Gunsmith, had told her during her apprenticeship with him, "Get used to that target on your back, because once it's there you can never get rid of it. You'll just have to defend it." That was what he and his friends—like Bat Masterson, Wyatt Earp and a man named Slocum—had been doing for years. It was the same for Wild Bill Hickok, until a backshooter managed to put a bullet right in the center. The same was true for Jesse James.

Clint Adams expected to die from a bullet that came to him in the front, probably from the gun of somebody faster. Roxy had not become that jaded, yet. She was too young. But she was pretty much on her way . . .

***

Her first encounter with the miners had been in front of the office, when she arrived. Her second was when they all headed for the mess hall, for supper.

"You wanna what?" Gus Jensen asked her.

"I want to eat with the men," she said. "Let them see me, and talk to me, if they want."

"You mean, today?" Riley, the engineer asked.

"I mean every day I'm here," she said, "Breakfast, lunch and supper."

"We only do breakfast and supper," Jensen said.

"That's fine," she said. "It'll give them time to see that I'm not going anywhere. And that I'm not afraid to be around them."

"You're gonna hear some harsh remarks," Riley warned her. "I mean, these are miners, men who've been working in a hole in the ground for months without seeing a woman."

"These men are worse than cowboys," Jensen said. "At least ranch hands can get to town once in a while, blow off some steam."

As they left the office and walked to the mess she asked, "So what do these men do to blow off steam?"

"Play cards, mostly," Jensen said.

"Fight, sometimes," Riley said.

"Gamble on who'll win," the foreman added.

"We got one fella who plays the guitar and sings," Riley said, "another plays the mouth organ. Sometimes they play together and the men sit around and listen."

"Doesn't sound so bad."

"Now that you're here," Jensen said, "they're gonna wanna dance."

"Oh God . . ." Riley said, shaking his head. "What a spectacle that'll be."

"I'm going to guess that you two fellas were educated in the East."

"Boston," Riley said, with a nod.

"New York," Jensen said. "I grew up there, on the dirty streets. Had to learn early on how to defend myself."

"I was born in the west," Riley said, "in Virginia City, but then I went to college in Boston."

"And these men?"

"They're from all over," Jensen said. "East, West, Ireland, China, England . . . we've got 'em all."

"And you hired them all?" she asked Jensen.

"Every one," he said. "Some I knew beforehand, some I interviewed and hired."

"And you feel you can vouch for them?"

"Every one."

When they reached the mess hall and entered, the men who were already seated turned and looked at her. And the whistles and catcalls started.

“Okay, okay, you animals, settle down,” Jensen said. “When everybody’s present, I’ll introduce the lady, but for now mind your manners.”

There were half a dozen long wooden tables, with benches on either side. She noticed that no one sat at the head of the tables at either end. She assumed that was so nobody could claim any sort of seniority, or authority over the others.

She walked with Jensen and Riley to one of the tables, which at the moment was half full. Some of the men there started licking their hands and smoothing their hair down in a vain attempt to improve their appearance. But all of them pretty much looked like they had just crawled out of a hole in the ground which, of course, they had.

Roxy sat with Jensen on one side, Riley on the other. Across from her three men grinned.

“Is this where you always sit?” she asked, in a low tone, actually leaning against Jensen so only he would hear her. She enjoyed both the heat and the solid feel of his body against her.

“Every morning and every evening,” Jensen said. “We all sit in the same spot.”

"Then you might as well start by introducing me to these three grinning fellas," she said.

"Boys," Jensen said to the three, "this is Roxy. Roxy, that's Biff on the left, Rex in the center, and on the right there is Angus."

"Angus McNab," the Irishman said, "of the highland McNabs, Ma'am. Happy to make yer acquaintance."

"You're a sight for sore eyes, Miss," Rex said, "if you don't mind me sayin' so."

"Not at all."

They were all strapping big fellas in their early or late thirties. As she looked around at the seated men, and the ones filing in, she saw that the miners varied from early twenties to early fifties, from short to tall, but all of them seemed fit. There wasn't a soft, fat belly among them. Some of them might have been ugly as hell, but these were all men, and at the moment, all of their eyes were on her.

She could feel the hunger.

Chapter Twenty

Jensen stood and made a short introduction, telling the men who she was, and why she was there. He assured them that if anyone wanted to get in her way, she would be able to handle them. A couple of men shouted that they wouldn't mind being handled by her, but Jensen cut off that kind of talk before it could spread.

"The lady works for Mr. Tabor, who is our boss," Jensen said. "I don't think I need to say more. Now you can eat."

Roxy's first surprise was at how good the food was. It was a thick, meaty beef stew served in bowls, with plenty of bread to soak it.

"This is thanks to Horace," Jensen said, when she commented on how good it was. "He wants his men to have the best of everything, and he puts his money to work."

The food was washed down with beer that was somehow ice cold.

"We keep it in kegs in a nearby cold stream," Riley told her. "It's always cold, because the water comes rolling down from further up."

After they had all eaten, the same servers came out carrying large coffee urns and filled everyone's mugs. It was rich and strong.

"What happens after they've eaten?" she asked. "Is it too late to go back down in the mines to work?"

"Yes," Jensen said. "The men go to the bunkhouse, or sit on a rock under a tree, or whatever they want to do to relax. In the morning, they'll be up at dawn and back down in the mines."

"And what do you do?" Roxy asked Jensen.

"I spend as much time in the office as I can before I have to go to the bunkhouse."

"And you?" she turned to Riley.

"I sit outside, under the stars, until it's time to turn in. The bunkhouse is always so noisy I can't think."

"Well then," she said, "that leaves me to spend time with you under the stars," she turned to Jensen, "or with you in the office."

"The choice is yours," Jensen said, "but I'll warn you, Riley talks about techniques of mining as much as he talks about the stars."

"I'll remember that."

As the men began to file out to go off to whatever relaxations they preferred, Riley stood up and said, "Excuse me. I'll probably be seeing you around camp."

"Yes, you will," she said.

He left with the other men. Before long, she was alone in the mess with Jensen, and the men who were cleaning up.

"Who's your cook?" she asked.

"A man Horace brought in from Denver," Jensen said. "He pays him very well."

"And tell me about Mr. Riley," she said. "Do you trust him?"

"You know," he said, "both Pinkerton men asked me the same question. I'm afraid I do."

"So you knew the men were Pinkertons," she said. "Did anyone else?"

"No, Horace sent word only to me, as he did about you."

"I see. And you didn't let anyone in on it?"

"No."

She stood up.

"What's on your schedule now?"

"Back to the office to do some work," he said. "You're welcome to join me."

"I think I'll walk around camp while it's still light," she said, "get the lay of the land."

"I can have someone go with you, show you around," he offered.

"No, that's all right," she said. "I'll make my own way around camp."

"Okay, but stay away from the mine shaft," he said. "They can be deadly if you don't know what you're doing. Uh, that is, unless you have mining experience?"

"None at all," she said.

"And if any of the boys give you trouble—"

"I'll take care of it myself," she said. "I wouldn't want to get anyone in trouble."

"Okay," he said, "but, uh, you won't, uh . . ."

"Shoot them? No. That's not why I'm here."

They left the mess together.

"I'll see you later," he said. "I should still be in the office when you wander over. But I'll vacate whenever you decide you want to turn in."

"That's nice of you, but I don't want to interfere with your work."

"You won't be," he assured her.

As Jensen walked away, she wondered if finding the guilty party was as easy as knowing that Jensen was the only one who had known who the Pinkertons were? She hoped not. Since he was so very handsome, she was looking forward to getting to know him a little better.

***

As she walked around camp, she made a point of keeping an eye out for the engineer, Riley. She had some questions she wanted to ask him, without Jensen around.

She exchanged nods with some of the men who were sitting around campfires, heading for or coming from the bunkhouse, none of whom made any remarks. She wondered how long that level of respect would last?

When she finally came across Riley, who was standing off to one side, staring at the sky and smoking a cigarette, she approached him.

"Oh, hello," he said, noticing her.

"I hope I'm not bothering you," she said.

"Not at all," he assured her. "I was just . . . thinking. Can I help you with anything?"

"One thing in particular," she said.

"And what's that?"

"Tell me, do you trust Gus Jensen?"

Chapter Twenty-One

Riley looked surprised by the question.

"Why would you ask me that?" he inquired.

"Because I asked him the same question about you," she said. "You are the two men running things up here, right? I need to know if you trust each other."

"And then you'll decide if you can trust us?"

"No," she said, "I'll decide that for myself after I've known the two of you a bit longer and observed you."

"You sound very educated for someone so young. Where did you go to school?"

"I grew up in Utah Territory," she said. "I left there when I was fifteen. My education has taken place since then, in the places I've been and the people I've met."

"A self-made woman," he said. "I admire that."

"Not so self-made," she said. "I've learned a lot from a lot of people."

"But you've really educated yourself," he said. "I think that's wonderful."

"Are you trying not to answer my question Mr. Riley?" she asked.

"Just call me Stan," he said.

"Stan," she said, "you're avoiding my question."

"I'm sorry. I trusted Gus until I found out about the Pinkertons."

"You didn't know they were Pinkertons?"

"No," he said. "Gus never told me."

"Do you think that was because he didn't trust you?" she asked. "Or because Mr. Tabor told him to keep it to himself?"

"A little bit of both, I guess," he said. "How did he answer this question?"

"He said he trusted you totally."

"Really?" Riley's eyebrows went up.

"Does that surprise you?"

"Frankly, yes," he said. "Well . . . I guess I trust him, then."

"So you don't think he's sabotaging things up here?"

"Oh, hell, not at all," he said. "You should've asked me that, first. This mine is Gus's baby, he'd never do anything to damage it."

"But he doesn't own a piece, does he?"

"A very small piece," Riley said.

"Ah, I didn't know that," she said. "Mr. Tabor told me Gus was the foreman. He never told me he was a partner."

"A very junior partner, but a partner nonetheless, yes," Riley said.

"Interesting."

"How do you intend to find out who *is* doing the damage?" he asked.

She didn't tell him she was going to wait for them to try to kill her. Instead, she said, "I'm going to watch and learn."

"Do you think one of the men here is involved?"

"It could be," she said. "Even though Gus doesn't seem to think so."

"I'm sure Gus told you he personally selected these men," Riley said. "To have one of them turn out to be a saboteur would be a crushing blow to him."

"I get that," she said.

"Is there anything else I can help you with?" he asked.

"Not right now. I'm just going to walk around and get the lay of the land."

"Alone?"

"I think I'll be safe enough."

"These men haven't seen a woman in . . . well a long time," he warned.

"I'll keep that in mind."

"And stay away from the mines, themselves," he warned. "They can be dangerous if you're not careful."

"So I've been told," she said. "I'll watch my step."

She started away, then turned back.

"I do have one more question," she said.

"What's that?"

"Do the men look up to Gus?"

"Oh yes," Riley said. "They're very loyal."

"Tell me, is there another man here that the other's look up to?" she asked. "Other than you or Gus?"

Riley accepted the compliment without acknowledging it.

"Tom Richter."

"And who's he?"

"One of the first miners Gus hired," he said. "They had worked together on some other jobs. He's been a miner for a long time."

"How will I know him?" she asked.

"Easy," Riley said. "He's the oldest man in camp. Tom's in his fifties, and his hair's going grey."

"I think I remember seeing him at supper," she said. "Thanks very much."

"Sure. If there's anything else I can do to help, just let me know."

"I will," she said. "I'm going to have to depend on you and Gus heavily."

"That's more than those poor Pinkertons did," he observed.

***

She spent the next hour walking around the camp, down by the stream Gus had mentioned, even stuck her head in the bunkhouse. The men there immediately invited her in, but she smiled at them, waved, and backed out. As it started to get dark, she headed for the office, but along the way she came upon three men standing together, talking, and realized one of them had to be Tom Richter.

"Excuse me," she said, interrupting them. "Are you Mr. Richter?"

The older man turned and looked at her with a smile that almost made him handsome, despite the lines in his face.

"I'm Tom Richter. What can I do for you?"

"Can we talk?" she asked. "I'm just heading for the office. Would you walk with me?"

"Stay here and talk to these guys or walk with you?" he said. "That ain't a hard decision to make, Miss." He turned to his companions. "See you guys later."

Chapter Twenty-Two

Roxy linked her left arm with his as they walked, figuring it would help break down any guard he might have had up.

"I'll say goodnight here," he said, as they reached the office.

"Thank you for walking me home."

"My pleasure."

She looked at the window, which showed the light burning inside.

"Do you ever work at night?" she asked.

"Nope," he said. "That's Gus's habit, not mine. I try to get as much sleep as I can."

"The bunkhouse must be loud."

"It's not so much a bunkhouse as a barracks," he said. "And yeah, it's loud. Even when those mugs are sleepin' there's a lot of snorin'. See you tomorrow, Miss Doyle."

"Roxy," she said. "Just call me Roxy."

"Goodnight, then, Roxy."

She watched him walk off toward the barracks, then mounted the steps and entered the office.

Gus looked up from the drafting table and smiled.

"Ready to turn in?" he asked.

"Only if you won't have a drink with me," she said. "You must have a bottle around here somewhere."

"I do," he said, "but it's only rotgut. I'm sure, working for Horace, you're used to his fine brandy."

"I don't like brandy," she said. "Beer and whiskey are what I drink."

"Okay, then."

He went to a cabinet, opened it and took out a half-filled bottle, then found two coffee mugs and poured.

"Here you go," he said, handing her one.

"Thank you. Did I interrupt your work?"

"No," he said. "As a matter of fact, I was just finishing up. How was your walk?"

"Good. I met a man named Tom Richter. The oldest man in camp, isn't he?"

"Tom may be fifty or so, but he's a hard worker. He's been a miner for over thirty years."

"He seems like a nice man."

"He is," Gus said, "and he's my main guy in the mines. The others respect him."

"And I spent some time with Stan Riley," she said. "We talked."

"Oh? About what?"

"About you, and him," she said. "It seems you trust each other."

"Well, that's good to know."

"And you trust Richter, right?"

"Completely."

"So there should be three men in camp I can count on," she said.

"Really?" he said. "Just because we trust each other means you'll trust us?"

"Well," she said, "I've got to start somewhere when I'm eliminating people."

"That's true," Jensen said, "but I'm telling you none of my men are involved in this."

"I understand you feel that way, Gus," she said. "But you have to understand my position."

"You need to suspect everyone."

"Right," she said, "so I'll start by eliminating you three, and go from there."

"I don't know what I can do to help," he said. "The Pinkertons wouldn't let me do a thing."

"Why not?"

"It was their attitude," he said. "Both of them. They were the experts, and all the amateurs had to step aside."

"But you're the closest to the situation," she said. "So instead of giving you a say so, they got themselves killed."

"That's about the size of it."

"Well then, let me give you something to think about, Gus," she said.

“What’s that?”

“Suppose you had to pick out two men in your camp who you’d suspect. Who would they be?”

“Aw, jeez—” he said.

“I know,” she said. “But give it some thought, will you? I’ll ask you again tomorrow.”

“Okay.” He put his mug down on top of a filing cabinet. “I’ll let you turn. Breakfast is at eight a.m.”

“And when do the men go into the mines?”

“At nine.”

“Then I’ll be able to go into the barracks after that.”

“To search?”

She nodded.

“Be my guest,” he said. “The Pinks did that, too. They didn’t find anything.”

“I’ll be looking with different eyes.”

“I’ll see you in the morning.”

After he left, she poured herself another drink and sipped it while searching the office. She may have said she trusted him, but she still wanted to have a look around—the drafting table, a small desk under a window, a closet, the file cabinet. She looked in all those places and didn’t find a thing.

When she finished, she wiped out her mug with a rag, then went and got his from the file cabinet. Before wiping his mug off with the rag, she put her lips to where his lips had touched it. He was a very handsome man, and she hoped she'd be able to trust him completely, eventually.

Then maybe they'd be able to get to know one another better—a lot better.

***

A man outside the office watched her from the small window he knew was above the desk. When she walked to the desk, he ducked down. When he looked up again, she was at the file cabinet. He watched her until she put down her bedroll and turned in for the night—keeping her gun very close.

Chapter Twenty-Three

When she got to the mess for breakfast, most of the men seemed to be there. Jensen and Riley were seated where they had been before, with the space between them vacant.

"Good morning, gents," she said, climbing onto the empty spot between them. She made sure to press her body against Jensen's, leaving a space between her and Riley.

"Good morning, Roxy," Riley said.

"How'd you sleep in the office?" Gus Jensen asked.

"Fine," she said "It's a little better on the floor than being outside on the ground . . . but—"

"But what?" Jensen asked.

She lowered her voice.

"There was a time when I had the feeling I was being watched."

"Well," he said, also lowering his voice, "we told you these men haven't seen a woman in some time. Maybe one or more of them snuck out to take a peek."

"Luckily," she said, "I slept with my clothes on. Which reminds me, where can I get a good wash?"

“Down at the stream,” he said, “but I’ll have to send someone with you to make sure no one watches you there.”

“Can it be you?” she asked Jensen.

“Sure,” he said, “but I have to warn you, the water is pretty cold.”

“I’ll make it quick,” she promised.

The servers came out with the food and they stopped talking and started grabbing . . .

***

After breakfast, Riley leaned across Roxy and asked Jensen, “Do you think I can get to the drafting table this morning?”

“No problem,” Jensen said. “I told Roxy I’d take her to the stream so she can wash, and I’d keep watch for her.”

“That’ll work,” Riley said.

As the servers began cleaning up, the three of them stepped outside. The men were all on their way to the mines.

“Well, I’ll see you two later,” Riley said. “Don’t do anything down by the stream that I wouldn’t do.”

“Now,” Roxy said, slipping her left arm through Jensen’s, “what do you suppose he meant by that?”

"He's just trying to be funny," Jensen said, "and he's not very good at it."

They stopped by the empty barracks to get Roxy a towel and some soap, and then walked to the stream, which was quite a ways from the camp.

"We usually have somebody come down here with a wheelbarrow and collect water," Jensen explained.

"It looks pretty shallow," she said, of the water that was flowing from the north.

"There's a deep patch over here that's good for bathing," he promised. "And it's sort of hidden behind some bushes."

He led her to it and said, "Here we are."

"What a beautiful spot," she said. "Do you come here often?"

"Actually," he said, "not at all. No reason to."

"No baths?"

"We have some tubs in camp," he said. "The men use them when the dirt on them gets too thick."

"Then I could have used one."

"Having you take a bath in camp would not be a good idea," he said. "Not the way you look."

"I suppose not," she said.

"So you go ahead, and take your time," he said. "I'll keep an eye out, although I'm sure nobody will come along. This is pretty remote."

"All right," she said. "Thanks."

She took the towel and soap and moved through the brush to the edge of the stream. As much as she wanted a bath, she didn't feel good about wading in and leaving her gun on shore. But then she found a spot deep enough so she could slide right in, and still be within reach of the gun.

She undressed, folded her clothes and set them down at the edge of the stream, then put the holster right on top of them. That done she slid right off the shore into the water, which came to her waist. She crouched down and used the soap on her face, neck, shoulders, breasts, torso, and her back as much as she could perch. She couldn't sit and soap her legs because the bottom was craggy. It was hard enough to keep from cutting her feet, she wouldn't have wanted to risk a lacerated butt. So she just reached into the water and rubbed her legs down vigorously. Then she soaped her hands, set the soap aside, and did her hair. All the while she was wondering if Jensen was keeping watch or watching her. Just in case he *was* watching, she stood and rinsed herself off languidly, rubbing her breasts and nipples with both palms. She felt herself getting excited, and was hoping he *was* watching.

Finally, she got out of the water and took her time drying off with the thin towel.

"Gus, are you there?" she called.

"I'm here," he said, sounding close by.

"Did anyone come along?"

"No," he said, "no one."

"And did you watch me?"

There was hesitation, then he said, "I'm sorry, it's been a long time for me, too."

"Well," she said, playfully, "if this place is as remote as you say it is, why don't you come and take a bath yourself?"

More hesitation.

"I'll wash your back."

She heard rustling, as if he was moving quickly, then when he came into view from behind the bushes, he was naked.

Chapter Twenty-Four

He was fit and muscular, and had a large cock that was already getting hard. Thankfully, his body was almost hairless. She hated men with thick body hair.

"Jesus," he said, staring as she set the towel aside so he could see all of her. He stared at her big breasts, topped by pink nipples that were hard from the cold water, and her lovely pale skin, still glistening as the air continued to dry her. The weather was mild, and she wasn't shivering now that she was drying off.

He came close to her and made a move as if to step into the water, but she stopped him by taking hold of his cock with one insistent hand. The move brought him up short and he stared into her eyes.

"After," she said, "we'll both wash up after."

She snaked her other hand behind his neck and brought his face down for a kiss. He wrapped his arms around her instantly and she allowed him to pull her up against his hot body as their mouths fused together hungrily.

She released her hold on his penis so she could run her hands up and down his strong back, only to end up cupping the cheeks of his powerful butt. If this was the kind of body working in the mines built, she was all for it.

He broke the kiss so he could run his mouth over her neck, shoulders and breasts, thrilling her when he centered his attention on her nipples, biting and sucking them. She'd had many men do this to her before, but most were clumsy about it. Gus Jensen seemed to know exactly what he was doing to send little waves of delight through her.

When he put one hand down between her legs, she was so hot and wet for him that his fingers slid right into her. At that point they both looked around for someplace to lie down, but it was all hard rocks or bushes.

"Wait . . ." he said, and slid his strong arms underneath her thighs so he could lift her up. She knew what he intended so she put her arms around his neck to take some of her own weight off his arms. He barely needed it, however, as he brought her down and impaled her on his long, hard cock. She was a big girl and had not been with many men who could've handled her this way.

Together they got her bouncing up and down on his penis. She grunted each time she came down on him, because he pierced her deeply with each thrust.

Roxy found the situation itself almost as exciting as their actions were. After all, anyone could have come along and found them. And they were precariously perched at the edge of the stream, with hard rocks and brambles around them. One tumble and they'd both end up the worse for wear.

Each time she came down on him she thought her body would explode, until finally it did, sending waves of pleasure all through her, as well as lights going off like lightning bolts in her brain . . .

. . . and then when he exploded into her, she almost screamed . . .

***

They staggered together into the stream, laughing, washing each other's back, and finally they were so excited, Roxy was so wet and Jensen was so hard against her that she had to climb atop him and fuck quickly and manically, again . . .

***

Roxy usually sent men packing after sex. She used them to scratch an itch after some time on the trail. She was raised not to value men beyond what she could use them for. She could count on the fingers of one hand—not including her thumb—the number of men she'd wanted to spend more time with after an initial coupling—the Gunsmith, Clint Adams, being the first to come to mind.

However, she thought that in the future, Gus Jensen might actually come to mind right after Clint . . .

"Oh my God," she said, as they dressed quickly, on the lookout for anyone who might have been watching. After all, why else would anyone come there, but to collect water, and Jensen assured her they had plenty, at the moment.

"The only way somebody would be watching," he said, "is if they followed us when we left, and right now they should all be in the mine, working." He got his boots on, straightened up and looked at her. "So if I did find a man watching us, I'd fire him on the spot."

She finished with her own boots, then completed buttoning her shirt as she faced him.

"What about Riley?"

"No, I couldn't fire him," he said, "We need him—but I'd knock him on his ass!"

"It looks like there won't be any need for that," she said, strapping on her gun. "Nobody's here."

She picked up the towel and the soap.

"I have to say," she said to him, "I've never been manhandled like that. You're a strong man."

"You're a powerful girl," he said, "as well as being beautiful. And I didn't want any of these brambles or hard rocks to scratch or bruise you."

"Well," she said, "it looks like we're both impressed."

"Believe me," he said, "I was impressed with you before this. Now I'm just . . . well . . ."

"I know," she said. "Me, too."

As they walked back, she realized that, right now, she *truly* hoped he wouldn't end up being involved in the sabotage.

Chapter Twenty-Five

The camp looked deserted to Roxy, and she commented on it.

"Riley will be in the office," he said "the cook's in the kitchen with his servers. Yeah, this is generally how the camp looks while the men are in the mine."

"I'd like to see some of the accident sites," she said.

"A couple of them are in the mine," Jensen said. "I'd have to take you down there."

"Okay," she said. "Why don't we start with the ones that weren't inside the mines?"

"We can do that," Jensen said. "There are a few things I have to do with Riley this morning, but how about this afternoon?"

"That'd be fine."

"What will you do 'til then?" he asked.

"If it's okay with you, I'll have a look at the barracks while the men are at work."

"Sure, that's fine with me," he said. "Maybe you'll find something the Pinkertons didn't."

"Like I said before," she reminded him, "I'm looking with different eyes."

"I'll find you after I've finished my business with Stan," he promised.

He mounted the steps and went into the office. Roxy watched every step he took, then when the door closed, turned and headed for the barracks.

***

The barracks were set up just like an army barracks, with bunks, and footlockers containing the men's personal belongings. As she strolled through the building, she checked underneath bunks and mattresses, not sure what she was looking for, but figuring she'd know it when she found it.

Some of the footlockers were locked, and some weren't. That didn't necessarily mean the owners of the locked ones had something to hide. This could have just been a personal preference—some locked them, and some didn't.

She opened the unlocked ones and found extra socks and pants, extra boots, some letters. There were guns or knives, in others she found things like rosary beads, Bibles, other religious artifacts indicating that the miners had a variety of different beliefs. But she found nothing incriminating.

"Find anything?"

She turned and saw Tom Richter standing in the doorway. She hoped he hadn't been there very long, because that would mean she hadn't noticed him.

"Not much," she said.

"Did you think you would?"

"Probably not," she said, "but I have to take every precaution."

He came into the building and pointed to one trunk in particular.

"Did you go through mine?"

"Yours is locked."

"Well, I can fix that." He walked to the trunk, leaned over and unlocked it. "There you go. Have a look."

Roxy decided to take him up on his offer. She went through it while he watched, but found nothing incriminating.

"How do you like my taste in clothes?" he asked.

"It's fine," she said.

"What do you think the rest of the boys would say or do if I told them I found you in here?" he asked.

"What are you doing here?" she asked. "I thought everybody was in the mine?"

"It's *mines*," he said. "Matchless is made up of different tunnels and caverns."

"All right," she said, "mines, then. Why aren't you in one?"

"We don't break for lunch," he said. "But we all get breaks, and we take them separately. Should be a few more of the boys along any minute."

"That's okay," she said. "I'm done in here."

"You sure?"

She walked to the door, turned back.

"You can tell them anything you want," she said. "I'll tell them I was here doing what Horace Tabor paid me to do. Seems to me as a man the others look up to, you'd be in favor of that."

"I'm in favor of you finding whoever is out to ruin Tabor," he said. "But you're lookin' in the wrong place. Nobody here benefits if the mine shuts down. What you have to find out is, who does."

"Thanks for defining my job for me, Mr. Richter."

"Just call me Tom," he said. "Everybody around here does."

"Thanks," she said. "I'll remember that."

She left the barracks, and as she walked across the compound saw three or four more miners heading for the building. They called out to her, invited her to visit them in the barracks any time she wanted to. She nodded and waved back to them, graced them with a smile to show she could take some good-natured ribbing.

She wondered about Tom Richter, though. How did a man of his age really feel about still working in a mine?

Wouldn't he be looking for some better way to spend his later years? A way to make himself some money for retirement?

***

As the four men entered the barracks, they saw Tom Richter sitting on his bunk.

"Hey, Tom," Ben Revere said, "we saw that red-haired girl outside, tried to get 'er to come on in with us. We coulda showed her a good time."

Richter looked at the men, laughing and poking each other. He stood up and headed for the door.

"She's lookin' for a lot more than a good time," he told them, as he went out.

Chapter Twenty-Six

If Richter was behind the sabotage, he could surely influence others to join him. But Roxy knew Gus Jensen would never go for that as a possibility. He had too much invested in the older man. In fact, she had the idea that Richter might be the man who first got Jensen into the business—a mentor. That would make suspecting him an even bigger stretch.

When she reached the office, she didn't go in. Instead, she walked around it, stopped at the window she figured was just above the desk. Studying the ground, she saw footprints, as if someone had been standing there, looking in. Were they spying on her the night before? Or was someone watching Jensen and Riley? From the size of the footprints, they could have belonged to any of the miners. The only person they looked too small to fit was Jensen, but then why would he be looking in his own window?

She made her way completely around the building until she was back in front, then went to the door. As she entered, the two men looked up from the drafting table.

"I'm sorry to interrupt," she said. "I know you're working, but then so am I."

"And you're working for the same man we are, so don't worry about it," Jensen said. "What can we do for you?"

"I'm thinking about Tom Richter."

"What about him?" Riley asked.

"He's been a miner for a long time," she said. "Do they usually last this long?"

"No," Jensen said, "but Tom's not the normal old miner."

"In what way?"

"He loves it down there," Jensen said. "and he's in top shape. As for actual work, he puts these younger guys to shame."

"What is it specifically that you were wondering?" Riley asked.

"Could it be possible he's tired of it, and is looking for a way out?"

"Not a chance!" Jensen said.

"Now wait," Riley said, "let her talk."

"What?" Jensen demanded. "You agree with her that it could be Tom behind all this sabotage?"

"I'm just saying let the lady talk."

Jensen fell silent, fuming.

"I'm not accusing him," she said, mostly to Jensen, "but he caught me in the barracks just now, and his attitude was . . . I don't know . . . smug."

"How so?" Riley asked.

"Like he knew I wouldn't find anything," Roxy said. "He even unlocked his footlocker for me."

"Maybe," Jensen said, "he did that because he's got nothing to hide."

"You're probably right, Gus," she said. "I'm just tossing it out there."

"Well, I'm tossing it back," Jensen said. "It's not Tom Richter. Jesus, I'd suspect me before I'd suspect Tom."

Roxy looked at Riley, who shrugged.

"Gus knows the man better than I do," he said.

"Okay, then," Roxy said. "It's not Tom."

"Stan," Jensen said, "Roxy wants to see some of the sabotage sites. Why don't you show her. I've got more work to do."

Roxy had the feeling she'd made Jensen too mad for him to spend time with her, right now.

"Sure, Gus," Riley said, coming around from behind the big table. "Come on, Roxy."

Jensen turned his attention to something on the table and didn't look at Roxy again, so she followed Riley out the door.

"I made him mad," she said.

"Don't worry about it. Tom Richter is a god to Gus, got him started years ago. They looked after each other."

"I figured," Roxy said.

As she followed Riley to the first sabotage site, she wondered if she should simply suspect both Gus and Richter. What if the older man did want to make himself some money to retire, and asked Gus for help? Would the younger man go along with it? She hated to suspect Jensen, but who'd be in a better position to cause mayhem than the foreman and his number one man?

***

Riley showed Roxy some scaffolding that collapsed for apparently no reason, injuring several men.

"I think we still have the wood somewhere, if you want to see it," he offered.

"I wouldn't know what I was looking at."

After that, there was a team of two horses that somehow got loose from the wagon they were pulling, and trampled two miners, injuring them both so badly they had not yet returned to work.

Then there was a flume that collapsed, supposedly under the weight of the water that was flowing through it, but there was no discernible reason for it.

"After that," Riley said, "Mr. Tabor brought in the first Pinkerton."

"And he was killed?"

"Yes."

"How?"

"A cave-in, which is the way a lot of miners meet their maker," Riley said.

"Could that have been an accident?"

"Ironically," Riley said, "it probably was. But then Mr. Tabor sent for a second Pinkerton."

"And how was he killed?"

"We found him face down in one of the mine shafts, stabbed in the back, with a pickaxe."

"Definitely not an accident," she said. "Have there been any accidents since then?"

"One last week, which is what brought Mr. Tabor to Leadville from Denver. He came up here to have a look at the operation, himself. He said he was going to hire security men to stand watch at night, but I guess he sent you, instead."

"If that's the case," she said, "it wasn't a smart move."

"You saying you can't fix this?"

"I can try," she said, "but I can't do that and stand watch. He should have hired a couple of security guards, anyway. How do you communicate with him?"

"We usually send someone to Leadville to send him a telegram in Denver or, if he's there, deliver it in person."

"Well, let's send him one and see if we can get a couple of security guards up here," she said. "That's what he should have gotten from the Pinkertons in the first place."

"Okay," he said. "We'll have to go back to the office."

"And after that," she said, "I want to see the mine shafts where the accident, and the murder, took place."

"That's no problem."

As they walked, she said. "Horace didn't tell me anything about a murder. Was the law up here?"

"There is no law up here," he said. "The law in Leadville said it wasn't in their jurisdiction."

"Then Tabor should get somebody federal up here," she said.

She decided that the message she would send him was going to be pretty long.

Chapter Twenty-Seven

In the office Riley allowed Roxy to sit at the desk and write out her message while he went to the drafting table with Gus Jensen. The foreman hadn't spoken to her or looked at her since she entered.

"That's it," she said, standing. "Who's the messenger?"

"We use two men," Riley said, "and they alternate." He turned to Jensen. "Whose turn is it?"

"I think it's Evans."

"I'll find him," Riley said.

"Wait for me," Roxy said, and this time it was she who wasn't looking at or talking to Jensen. If he wanted to sulk, then he wasn't the man she thought he was. "I want to see those mine shafts after we give him this message."

"Let's go, then."

They walked to the door, still with Roxy and Jensen not even exchanging a glance.

"How long is he going to sulk?" she asked Riley, as they looked for Evans.

"He'll get over it," Riley said. "You're just doing what Tabor paid you to do."

"Thanks."

"There's Evans," Riley said, pointing to a man who was outside the mess building. "We use him for odd jobs, like serving at breakfast and supper, and delivering messages."

The small, bandy-legged man saw them approaching and stared. Roxy thought he was in his twenties until they got closer and saw that he was over thirty.

"Evans, time for you to take a ride to Leadville," Riley said.

"It's about time," Evans said, looking not at Riley, but Roxy. "I been needin' to get off this mountain."

"Well, you can get off, deliver the message, wait for an answer, and come right back up here," Riley said.

"I'll do that," Evans said, "right after I have a beer and a steak. And maybe a woman."

"Don't take too long," Riley said, handing him the message. "We need a quick reply."

Evans put the message in his pocket.

"I'll saddle one of the horses."

"Aren't you going to read the message?" Roxy asked.

"No," he said, "it's my job to deliver it, not to read it."

"But you don't even know who to deliver it to."

Now the man looked at Riley and smirked.

"We only deliver messages to one man," he said. "In person if he's in Leadville, or by telegram if he's in Denver."

"All right, then," she said. "You better get going."

"Yes, Ma'am."

As he walked away quickly, Roxy turned to Riley.

"How long will he be away?" she asked.

"He'll be back tomorrow."

"Then he'll have to eat, drink and rut quickly."

"Evans does everything quickly," Riley said. "He has a lot of energy. The other man we use, Walters, is bigger, slower and—I hate to say it—dumber."

"Then I'm glad I managed to get Evans," she said. "How about a look at those mine shafts?"

"If you don't mind remarks from the men, we go can right now," he said.

"I can handle a few remarks," she said. "Lead the way."

***

Riley gave Roxy a hard hat and took her Stetson from her. He set it aside, and they went down the first shaft.

She heard the sound of voices, shovels and pickaxes as they got closer to the action. When the men saw her, they were true to Riley's word, making remarks and whistling.

"That's enough," Riley snapped. "Keep working."

They all bowed their heads and got back to work.

"This way," Riley said, leading her down another tunnel.

"Why is nobody working here?" she asked, as they walked.

"This tunnel has played out," he said, "but this is where we found the murdered Pinkerton."

"Where, exactly?"

"At the very end of the tunnel. The other one died in a cave-in. We can't get to that site."

They kept walking until the tunnel ended. She saw a stain on the ground that could have been dried blood.

"Here," he said. "Face down, in a pool of blood."

"Did anybody see him come in here?"

"No," Riley said, "or not that they're saying."

She turned and looked at him.

"Why do I get the feeling that you don't trust all these men as much as Gus does?"

"Like we told you," Riley said, "Gus hired them all, I didn't. He's very loyal."

"I saw that when I accused Tom Richter."

"Let's go back outside," Riley said. He didn't look very comfortable.

"Are you nervous?" she asked.

"I'm an engineer," he said, "not a miner. I don't spend as much time in these tunnels as they do. I—I like fresh air."

"All right, then," she said, "let's go outside and get some."

He led her back up the tunnel, past the working men again, and out into the light and air. When they got there, he stopped and took a deep breath.

"Are you all right?" she asked.

"I'm fine," he said. "Is there anything else?"

"Not much I can do until your man, Evans, gets back," she said. "I want to know if Tabor's going to send those security men."

"So what will you do in the meantime?"

"You know what?" she asked. "I think maybe, just for tonight, I'll be the security man."

Chapter Twenty-Eight

She ate supper with the men again, but this time she sat on the end, with Riley between her and Gus Jensen. The foreman still seemed to be pouting about her mention of Tom Richter as a suspect. When the men filed out after eating, Jensen went with them, leaving Roxy and Riley there, still drinking coffee.

"Seems like Gus doesn't want to talk to me anymore," she commented.

"Give him 'til tomorrow," Riley said. "I'll talk to him."

"No, leave him be," Roxy said. "If I need to speak to him, I'll make sure he answers. For now . . . just let him alone."

"Whatever you say."

"I'll be awake tonight, and moving around the camp," she said. "I want to see what this place is like at night. I also want to figure out where to place the security men, if Tabor sends them."

"Do you think they'll take orders from you?"

"In my message I told Tabor to let them know, in no uncertain terms, that I'm in charge."

"Let's hope he does it, then." He stood up. "I have to go back to the office. I'll see you before I turn in, in case you need anything else."

"Okay," she said, "thanks."

***

She preferred the idea of staying awake all night instead of having to go into the office and see Gus Jensen's pouty face again before he left and turned it over to her to sleep in.

She thought about their activity down by the stream and felt stupid. Letting a handsome face, set of broad shoulders and a big tallywacker distract her made her feel like a foolish female—and she hated that. She preferred the Roxy who used men and discarded them. She didn't ever want to revert to that fifteen-year-old girl being controlled by her foster father and brother.

She was taking back the control she had temporarily lost.

The footprints outside the office window were stuck in her mind. That and the feeling she was being watched the first night. Somebody in that camp was guilty, no matter what Gus Jensen thought of his men.

She walked around the camp in the expiring light, as the men began to file into the barracks to rest or turn in for the evening. Or whatever they did on their own time.

She peered in the window, not having to stand on her toes to do so. She'd probably be able to eliminate some of the men as being too short, but there were easily thirty men or so working the mines. She couldn't stand them in a line and measure them all.

She crouched down and studied the boot tracks for some feature that might help—a worn sole, a chipped heel, something. But the tracks were smooth, and she had an idea that Gus Jensen insisted that Tabor make sure his men had new boots often. These tracks probably matched twenty or twenty-five men, except for those who were very small, or very large. That meant average, and that word usually matched the majority.

While it was still light, she decided to find herself a perch, or a hidey-hole, someplace to light and sit during the night, when she wasn't walking around. She encountered two men behind the barracks, who were standing close together, deep in conversation. As she got closer, she saw that one of them was Tom Richter. The other was just one of the miners she recognized from the supper table.

As she approached, the miner looked at her, then as Richter said something to him, the other man hurried away.

"Secrets, Tom?" she asked.

"Men can have secrets without being saboteurs, Miss Doyle," the older man said.

"That's true," she agreed.

"What did you do to Gus?" he asked. "It looked to me at supper like you two had a lover's spat."

"Just a minor falling out over someone I gave my opinion about, suggesting they might be a suspect."

"Well," Richter said, "Gus is very loyal to his men. Which one did you mention?"

"It happened to be you."

"Oh." He laughed.

"What's so funny?"

"If I told you," he said, "it wouldn't be funny anymore."

And he walked away.

Chapter Twenty-Nine

Later that night, after darkness fell and all the miners were asleep in their barracks, Roxy found tables set up behind the mess building. She assumed when there were more miners than there were at that moment, they'd sit outside and eat.

But for now, it was a place she could settle, and consider her options for the night. Clint Adams had taught her that she was more than a gun and could do anything she wanted if she set her mind to it. She had no training in security or detective work, but at one time had been offered a job by Robert Pinkerton, who felt she had a natural affinity for the work.

Tonight she'd apply that affinity to the situation at the mine. She walked around the quiet compound in the dark, where torches had been lit every so often, then returned to her seat behind the mess, then walked again. She identified several places where a security guard could be stationed—certain mine tunnels and shafts. It would probably take a team of six guards to insure the safety of the entire operation, but how much would that cost Horace Tabor?

She didn't have any idea how willing he was to spend money. So far what he had spent on her was negligible, considering his wealth and the size of his Matchless Mine. Would he spend money on a cadre of security guards if she suggested it to him? Or would he risk more lives by trying to save money?

She'd know more when Evans came back with a reply from her message.

She was able to catch a few winks of sleep in between her walks around the camp. When the sun started coming up over the far mountain peaks, she walked to the stream to wash her face and hands. By the time the sun was out, she was feeling pretty good for having been up most of the night.

She was the first one in the mess for breakfast, so early in fact that she heard them preparing the food. When one of the servers came out to start setting up the tables, he looked surprised to see her. He was a young man, early twenties, and he recovered quickly enough to speak to her.

"Good-mornin', Miss," he said. "Can I bring you some coffee while you're waitin' for everyone to get here?"

"That'd be great, thanks."

As he went into the kitchen, it occurred to her that she really hadn't met anyone who worked there, especially the cook. She decided she'd do that after breakfast was over.

The young man came back with a mug of coffee.

"What's your name?" she asked.

"Oh, I'm Tommy."

"Thanks for the coffee, Tommy. I'm Roxy."

"Um, I know who you are, Miss," he said.

"Then call me Roxy."

"Oh, okay Roxy."

"Tommy, after breakfast will you take me to the kitchen and introduce me to the other servers, and the cook?"

"Oh, sure I will."

"Thanks." She saluted him with the mug.

The coffee did her much good and woke her even more by the time the men began filling the tables.

When Gus Jensen and Stan Riley came in, the foreman nodded, and the engineer said, "Good-morning. How was your night?"

They sat on either side of her again, but she kept some space between herself and Jensen, this time.

"It was fine," she said. "I got a lot of thinking done. Depending on what your man Evans brings back to us, I have a lot of suggestions for Horace."

"Will you be going back to Leadville to talk to him about them?" Jensen asked.

She turned her head and looked at him. She had the feeling he was as sorry about their romp at the stream as she was and wanted her to leave.

"I don't know," she said. "It will depend on what his message reply says."

"Have you found out anything helpful yet?" Jensen asked.

"Yes," she said.

"Like what?"

"Like the fact that some men aren't what I thought they were," she said.

He turned his attention to his breakfast, and Riley chuckled.

***

Tommy kept his word and after breakfast, took Roxy into the kitchen—which was just a big empty room with a table and a stove.

"This is Ken, that's Lloyd. And this here's our cook, Dusty."

Ken and Lloyd were young men like Tommy, but Dusty was an older gent with a bulging stomach and skin that was smooth, pink and sweaty.

"That was a fine breakfast," Roxy told him. "In fact, all the meals I've had since I got here have been great."

“Thank ya,” Dusty said, “it helps that Mr. Tabor makes sure I got good ingredients.”

“How often do you get deliveries, up here?”

“Every two weeks a buckboard pulls in with a load,” Dusty told her.

“Is it always the same men making the deliveries?” she asked.

“Pretty much,” Dusty said. “Comes from the mercantile in Leadville, and they usually send the same two fellas.”

“So you know them pretty well?”

“I seen ’em every two weeks for the past I don’t know how many months,” Dusty said, “but that don’t mean I know ’em real well.”

“What about the deliveries?” she asked. “Have they ever been hit?”

“Robbed, you mean?” Dusty asked. “Naw, it always gets here on time.”

“When is it due again?” she asked.

“Probably a week.”

“And when was the last . . . accident?”

Dusty looked at the three servers.

“A week ago?” Tommy asked.

“Yeah, about a week,” Dusty agreed. He looked at Roxy. “You don’t think—”

"I don't know what to think, yet," she said. "Thanks for talking to me."

"Sure thing."

She turned, left the kitchen and the building.

"There you are," Riley said, coming up on her.

"You looking for me?"

"We've got something you should see."

"Lead on," she said.

Chapter Thirty

Riley led Roxy behind the office, where the leanto with her horse was. It was also where the camp kept their two horses. There should have been one there now, since Evans had ridden the other to Leadville. But as they approached, she saw Gus Jensen standing next to a saddled horse.

"Is that—"

"Yes," Jensen said, "the horse Evans was riding. There's blood on the saddle."

"Damn it!" Roxy swore.

She approached the horse and saw the blood.

"Looks like somebody might have shot him out of the saddle," Riley said.

"The question is," she said, "did they do it when he was on his way to Leadville, or on the way back. Have you looked through the saddlebags?"

"Not yet," Jensen said. "We thought you'd like to do that."

"I would, thanks," she said.

The two men stood aside while she went through both saddlebags. In one she found the message she had written for Horace Tabor—undelivered.

"Looks like they got him on the way," she said.

"Damn!" Jensen swore. "Evans was a good man. Now we've lost another one." He turned on Roxy. "And on your watch, this time."

"Oh, come on Gus," Riley said. "She couldn't very well ride along with him, could she?"

"Why are you standing up for her?" Jensen demanded. "I'm going to take this horse out and look for Evans. Maybe he's out there, hurt."

"This had to have happened yesterday," Roxy said. "By now he's dead."

"Then why did the horse just come back today?" Jensen asked.

"It could have been wandering around out there all night," she said. "The animal is lucky it didn't injure itself. But it is tired."

"Then I'll saddle the other one," Jensen said. "Or yours."

"I don't think so, Gus," she said. "I can't allow you to go traipsing around by yourself."

"Then you come with me," Jensen said.

She hesitated, then said, "That might not be a bad idea. Okay, you saddle the other one, and I'll saddle mine."

They moved quickly, he taking the saddle from one mount and putting it on the other, she saddling her own.

Jensen took a moment to wipe Evans' blood off the saddle with a rag.

"You look after things here, Stan," Roxy said. "We won't stay out long."

"Long enough to find him!" Jensen snapped.

Roxy looked at him.

"I just want to see if I can pick up a blood trail," she said. "We can't ride all the way to Leadville looking for him."

As they started off, Jensen said, "Wouldn't you figure they hadn't gone halfway? I mean, the horse came back here."

"The horse returned here because this is where it's fed," she said. "They could have been right outside of Leadville, it still would've come back here. In fact, that would explain why it didn't return yesterday."

There was only one trail to ride down from the mountain, and, as they took it, Roxy didn't see any blood.

"Could the horse have come another way?" she asked.

"There is no other way."

"Then there wasn't enough blood on the saddle to drip off and leave a trail."

"So maybe he's not dead."

"If he was shot from the saddle, then he would've bled out on the ground."

"If he hung onto the saddle, he could've ridden a ways," Jensen reasoned. "But would he have headed back here or kept going to Leadville."

"Now that would depend on whether or not he had gone halfway when he was shot."

They continued to ride, hoping to find a live Evans on the side of the road. But after they had ridden several hours, there was nothing.

"We'd better head back," she said.

"He could still be out here somewhere, maybe hurt," Jensen argued.

"Then when we get back, take a few miners out to scour the mountain."

"I can't do that."

"Why not?"

"That would be taking them away from their work," he said, "Mr. Tabor wouldn't like that."

"How would he know?"

"I send him a short report every month, with one of the messengers."

"Short enough to be sent in a telegram?"

"Well, yeah. You know, like 'things are okay,' or 'another act of sabotage.'"

"Or 'a Pinkerton's dead?'"

"Exactly."

"We better turn around, Gus," she said.

"But why?"

"There could still be a shooter out in these rocks around us," she said.

"Are you worried they'll shoot you?" he asked.

"No," she said, "I'm worried they'll shoot you, and then I'll have to explain to Horace Tabor why I brought his foreman out here and made a target of him."

Now suddenly Jensen looked concerned, his eyes darting about the mountain.

"Okay," he said, finally, "let's head back."

They turned their horses and headed back up the mountain.

Chapter Thirty-One

They got back before dark, which suited Roxy. The last thing she wanted was for one of the horses to step badly, throwing one of them.

Evans' exhausted mount was in the leanto. Roxy and Jensen unsaddled their horses in silence. If they weren't talking about finding Evans, they weren't talking at all.

"I have to go to the office," Jensen said, when the horses were tended to.

"I'll come with you," she said.

They walked together.

"Should we tell the other men about Evans?" he asked.

"Did anyone other than you and Riley see the horse return here?" she asked.

"No."

"Then let's just keep it between the three of us for a while longer," she suggested.

"Among," he said.

"What?"

"Keep it 'among us,'" he said. "That's what you say when there's more than three. 'Between us' is for two people."

"Well," she said, "I'm continuing my education."

As they entered the office Riley, turned with his eyes wide and inquiring.

"Anything?"

"Nothing," Jensen said.

Riley looked at Roxy.

"He could've been shot near Leadville," she explained. "The horse still would've returned here."

"If we could get a message to Leadville—" Riley started.

"We'd have to send your other messenger," Roxy said, "but then he could get shot, also."

"But by who?" Jensen asked.

"And how would they know Evans was going to Leadville?" Riley asked.

"Somebody from here must've known," Roxy said. "They went out there to stop him from delivering it."

"Because it was going to bring security guards here," Jensen said.

"Who knew about the message other than the three of us?" Roxy asked.

They all looked at each other, and then Roxy said, "Evans. He must've told somebody he was going."

"And why," Riley said.

"Or," Jensen said, "it was one of us."

"Only you've both convinced me to trust the two of you," Roxy said.

"That's right," Jensen said, staring at her, "but can we trust you?"

"Horace Tabor does," she said.

"Yeah, but we only have your word for that."

"That's not true," Riley told Jensen. "We got a message from Mr. Tabor giving her his backing. He trusts her."

Jensen firmed his jaw and kept quiet.

"So we have to figure Evans told somebody what he was doing," Roxy said. "But who? Who are his best friends?"

Jensen and Riley exchanged a glance.

"Neither of you know?" she asked.

"I don't keep track of who's best friends with who," Jensen said.

"Then I'll have to ask around," she said. "Or maybe I'll just ask Tom Richter.'

"He'll probably know," Riley said.

"We missed supper," she said. "Think we can get something at the mess?"

"Come on," Riley said. "I didn't eat, either."

The three of them walked to the mess, where Jensen convinced Dusty to feed them.

***

Once they had eaten, they split up, Jensen and Riley going back to the office. Roxy went in search of Tom Richter.

She went to the barracks, which was so noisy she could hear the voices outside as she approached. She was surprised that the men had a lot of energy after working in the mines all day. She wondered if she just stuck her head in what she'd see. Some of the men might've been down to their skivvies, or less. Not that she would've minded seeing some naked men, but they might have objected.

"Hello!" she shouted, banging her fist on the door, which was open. "Anybody?"

"Well, look who it is," a man said, as he stuck his head out. "What can we do for you, little lady? You wanna come inside and party a little?"

"Maybe later," she said. "Is Tom Richter in there?"

"He sure is, but he ain't exactly dressed for company," the man said.

"Would you ask him if he'd step out here and talk to me?" she asked. "I won't keep him long."

"Lady," the man said, "none of these fellas would care how long you kept 'em. Hey, Tom!"

He pulled his head in and she could hear him calling out to Richter that there was a lady asking for him.

Richter came to the door, bare-chested but, thankfully, still wearing his trousers and boots. For a man his age

Roxy thought he was in fine shape, with a chest that looked like it had been cut from a slab of concrete.

"Figured it was you, since you're the only lady in camp," he said. "What can I do for you?"

"Can we take a stroll?" she asked.

"If you don't mind bein' seen with me like this," he said.

"I don't mind, at all."

"Then let's go."

Chapter Thirty-Two

They walked away from the barracks with some of the men sticking their heads out the door, or a window, and hooting at them.

"Don't mind them," Richter said. "They're young and stupid."

"That's okay," she said. "I'm used to that kind of thing."

"Yeah, I guess you would be."

"What's that mean?"

"You're beautiful," he said. "You probably have men actin' stupid around you all the time."

"Well, yeah . . ."

"Probably some old codgers like me, too," he added.

"You're not that old."

He laughed.

"Oh, I know that," he said. "I just figured you thought I was old."

"I don't," she said. "You look like you're in fine shape."

"Oh, I could keep up with you," he said, "and teach you a thing or two."

She turned her head and studied him.

"Hey," he said, "I didn't mean no offense."

“None taken,” she said. “I was just thinking you’re probably right.”

“About what, exactly?”

“About showing me a thing or two.”

“Well,” he said, “you just have to say the word.”

That hung in the air between them for a few more steps.

“Okay, well, did you have somethin’ to ask me?”

“It’s about Evans,” she said. “Do you know who his friends are?”

He frowned.

“Evans. Because they use him as a messenger, he’s never down in the mines. You might check with Windham.”

“Windham?”

“He’s the other messenger,” Richter said. “They spend some time together, but neither of them seems particularly friendly with the miners.”

Roxy had no idea where they were walking to, but Richter knew every nook and cranny of the camp. She suddenly realized they were in a pretty deserted area.

“Where are we?” she asked.

“We’re behind one of the mine tunnels,” he said. “Nobody ever comes back here.”

“Is that right?”

He turned to face her in the waning light. In fact, it was getting darker by the minute.

"What did you have in mind, Mr. Richter?"

"Do you have anything to do right now?" he asked.

"I'm just planning on talking with this Windham you told me about."

He stepped closer, pushing her up against the back wall of the mine. Almost in self-defense she put both of her palms against his chest, which was just as solid as it looked. She found herself rubbing her hands over his nipples, which were hard.

He leaned in to run his mouth over the smooth skin of her neck. At the same time, he unbuttoned her shirt so that her breasts fell into his hands. His fingertips felt rough from working in the mines all those years, but as he touched her nipples, she felt a thrill, as he seemed very knowing with his hands.

He worked his mouth down from her neck to her shoulders, then over the upper slopes of her breasts. His fingertips abandoned what they were doing, as his hands moved to cup her breasts, while his mouth and tongue were now doing wonderful things to her nipples. For a man who spent so many years in the mines, he certainly seemed to know what to do with a woman.

He moved his mouth up again, and this time he covered her mouth with his in a hot, feverish kiss. She put her arms around him and ran her hands over his powerful back.

"This isn't the place," he said, "or I'd take you right here and now."

"Why don't you?" she asked.

He looked around, but before he could make up his mind, her hands were on his trousers, unbuttoning them and reaching inside. One hand gripped his hard cock, while the other pushed his pants down over his hips, so that they fell around his boots.

She dropped to her knees, then, and took his hard penis into her mouth. He moaned as she began to suck him, her head bobbing back and forth as his cock stood out straight and long, rather than curving up as many did.

He might have been shorter and older than Gus Jensen, but in other ways he was bigger and better.

Richter groaned as Roxy ran her hands up and down the backs of his thighs while she continued to suck him. She felt maybe she was showing the older man a thing or two, instead of the other way around. But even while he was shooting hard and strong into her mouth, she was hoping they'd get to a bed in the near future.

"Jesus," he said, as she stood back up.

"You better get those pants pulled up," she said, "before somebody sees your white ass sticking out."

Even though he'd said nobody ever came back there, he hurriedly pulled his pants up. At the same time Roxy worked on the buttons of her shirt.

"You're quite a man, Tom Richter," she said. "We've got a date in a hotel room in the future."

"You're on," he said. "I didn't get to show you what I wanted to show you."

"Don't you worry about it," she said, licking her lips, and then wiping the corners of her mouth with her fingertips, "you showed me plenty."

When his trousers and her shirt were buttoned, they headed back toward the center of camp.

Chapter Thirty-Three

When they got back to the barracks, Richter was about to call out for Windham, but Roxy stopped him.

"Tell me about him, first."

"Not much to tell," Richter said. "He's young, not built for the mines. He's tall and gangly, so Gus decided to use him to run messages to Leadville."

"Did he and Evans discuss what they were doing?" she asked.

"Did they?" Richter said. "Is there somethin' you're not tellin' me?"

She grabbed his arm and steered him away from the barracks, again.

"Evans' horse came back without him. There was blood on the saddle," she said. "We sent him to Leadville with a message from me, telling Tabor he needed to send some security guards up here."

"So somebody killed him before he got there?"

"That's how it looks," she confirmed. "Gus and I rode out to take a look, see if we could find him, but no luck."

"So he could still be out there."

"Anything's possible."

"So what do you want to ask Windham?"

"We figure Evans told somebody what he was doing," she said. "And that person either did something about it, or told somebody else."

"If Windham rode out to shoot Evans, we would've missed him, wondered where he was," Richter said.

"Good point."

"And the same is true of anyone else in camp."

"Then he might've gone out and told somebody else."

"You mean, somebody who's out there," Richter said, "waitin' for another chance to sabotage us."

"Right."

"Well," Richter said, "you can't just ask 'im, can you?"

"No," she said, "maybe I'll just talk to Windham about Evans, and see if anything slips out."

"Okay, if he's in the barracks, I can send 'im out to you."

"Thanks, Tom."

"No," Richter said, with a grin, "thank you, Roxy."

She took a swipe at him as he headed back to the barracks.

***

Roxy watched as the gangly young man came out after several minutes. He looked around, spotted her and walked over, glassy-eyed. He was either curious, or simply enamored.

"Tom says you wanna talk to me, Miss?" he said in a high, squeaky voice.

"Yes," she said, "it's about your friend, Evans?"

"W-what about 'im?"

"Well, you probably know why I'm here in camp," she said. "Everybody probably knows by now."

"Yeah, you're tryin' to find out who killed them Pinkertons, and who's causin' accidents."

"Not accidents," Roxy said, "deliberate sabotage."

Windham's glassy eyes widened even further.

"You think Donnie's behind that?"

"Donnie?" she asked. "Is that Evans' first name?"

"Yeah."

"And what's your first name?"

"Barry."

"Well, Barry, I'm just wondering how well you really know Donnie?"

"I know him real good."

"And when you each get sent to Leadville with a message, do you tell the other one about it?"

"Well, sure. But ya gotta understand, we don't always read 'em, so we don't know what they say."

Roxy didn't like that. This all depended on Evans reading the message and telling somebody what it said.

"Did Evans tell you this time what it said?" she asked.

Windham hesitated.

"Will he get in trouble if he did?"

Since Evans couldn't get into any more trouble than he was probably in right at that moment, she said, "No."

"Then yeah, he told me," Windham said. "He read it just before he left and told me what it said. I guess we'll be havin' security guards up here pretty soon."

"Maybe not."

"You mean Mr. Tabor might not pay for them?" he asked. "He probably will."

"No," Roxy said, "I mean the message never got delivered. Donnie's horse came back in today without him, and the message is still in the saddlebag."

"What? What happened?"

"We don't know," Roxy said, "but there was blood on the saddle."

"Jesus!" Windham said. "We better go out and look for him."

"We did, but he could be anywhere on this mountain or nearer to Leadville."

"So whataya gonna do, then?"

"Well first, Barry," Roxy said, "I wanted to find out who he told, because we figure he told somebody who shot him out of his saddle."

"What?" Now Windham's eyes filled with tears, making them even more glassy. "You think I did it?"

"I don't know, Barry," Roxy said. "Did you?"

"Hell, no! Donnie's my friend."

"Okay then," she said. "did Donnie tell anyone else what he was doing?"

"He wouldn't," Windham said. "We weren't even supposed to tell each other."

"So you don't think Donnie told anybody else?"

"Hello, no!"

"Then Barry," Roxy said, "that only leaves you. Who did you tell?"

Chapter Thirty-Four

"W-what?"

"You heard me," she said. "If Donnie didn't tell anybody, then you must've."

Barry Windham started looking around, as if he was waiting for help.

"Barry," she said, "come on . . ."

Windham bit his lip, then said, "I—I think I'd rather talk to the boss."

"Gus? Or Mr. Tabor?"

"No, I mean Gus," Windham said.

"Then let's go and find him," Roxy said.

***

They found Jensen and Riley still in the office, even though darkness had fallen. Both men turned to face the door as Roxy and Windham entered.

"What's going on?" Jensen asked.

"Barry has something he wants to talk to you about," Roxy told Gus Jensen.

"What is it, Barry?" Jensen asked.

"I'd rather just t-talk to you, Mr. Jensen," Windham said.

"Look, Barry," Jensen said, "anything you can say to me you can say in front of Stan and Roxy."

Windham thought that over, then said, "Yeah, okay, boss."

"So start talking," Jensen said, somewhat impatiently.

"Go ahead, Barry," Roxy said, softer and with more patience, "we're listening."

"Before Donnie left yesterday," Windham said, "he read the message and then told me about it."

"So if he's not dead," Jensen said, "we'll fire him."

"Go on, Barry," Roxy said.

"I don't like the idea of security guards," Windham said. "Strangers standing around with guns? It makes the camp sound like some kind of prison."

He stopped, and Riley said, "I can understand that, Barry."

"Can you?" Windham said, hopefully. "Because that'll make this a whole lot easier."

"Sure," Riley said, "go on."

"Well," Windham said, "it's more than me that don't want guards up here. There's a few of us."

"So you told them what the message said?" Jensen asked.

"Um, yeah, I did," the young man said, then rushed and added, "but I don't think any of 'em did anything to Donnie."

"Barry," Roxy said, "that's going to be up to me to find out. And that means I'll need their names."

Windham looked at Jensen.

"If I give her their names, she'll kill them," he complained. "That's what she does."

"Don't be an idiot," Riley said, before Jensen could respond.

"That's her reputation, ain't it?" Windham asked, looking at Roxy with frightened eyes. "She might even kill me."

"She's not going to kill anybody, Barry," Jensen said. "I guarantee it."

"You can't believe every reputation, son," Riley said. "They're all exaggerated by the newspapers."

"Well, come on, man!" Jensen said. "The names."

Windham continued to hem-and-haw, but eventually all three of them convinced him he was better off naming names.

They got him seated in a chair and stood around him.

"All right, Barry," Roxy said.

"Sanderson," Windham said, "McDermott, Salazar... and Patrick."

Roxy looked at Jensen and Riley.

"Got that?"

"We've got it," Riley said.

"Turn in, Barry," Jensen said, "and don't talk about this to anyone. Got it?"

"I got it, boss."

He stood up, but before he could leave, Roxy grabbed his arm.

"If you do talk," she said, "we'll all find out if I'm as good as my reputation."

He nodded jerkily and rushed out the door.

Roxy turned to the two men.

"What about those names?"

"It can't be," Jensen said. "I interviewed those men, and hired them, personally. I've known two of them for years."

"All he's saying is that they didn't want security guards," Riley reminded him.

"So what did they want?" Roxy asked. "Saboteurs to have free reign?"

Both men looked at her.

"It would only have taken one of them," she went on. "One to pull the trigger, or to contact the man who did."

"But which one?" Riley asked.

"That's what I'm going to have to find out," she said, "before there are any more . . . accidents."

"So you don't think we should send another messenger to Leadville?" Riley asked. "This time sending someone with him?"

"No," she said, "we don't need to do that."

"Why not?" Jensen asked. "Have you given up on the security guard idea?"

"For now, yes."

"You have a new plan?" Riley asked.

She nodded.

"All we need to do," she said, "is let it be known that we *are* sending another messenger to Leadville."

"And then what?" Jensen asked.

"And then," she answered, "we wait."

Chapter Thirty-Five

Roxy hoped that Windham was scared enough to keep his mouth shut.

Jensen and Riley left her in the office to spend the night, so after they left, she rolled out her bedroll. She didn't see any point to spending another night awake. Things seemed to be starting to happen, with Evans missing or dead. Tomorrow she'd put her plan into effect, and then sit back and wait. It was like Clint Adams always told her, she'd have a bullseye on her back. Why should this time be any different?

She made sure the door was locked, took a quick look at the window above the desk before stretching out to sleep fitfully, with her gun and holster still around her waist.

***

At breakfast, she sat between Jensen and Riley and again discussed the plan in low tones. Actually, they didn't much care if they were overhead. They wanted word to get out that they were sending another messenger to Leadville to arrange for security guards.

"Who should we send?" Jensen asked, as if they were really discussing it.

"We've only got one messenger left," Riley said, "so we might as well send Windham."

"Alone?" Jensen asked.

"I'll go with him," Roxy said, loudly.

"Then you might as well deliver the message," Jensen said.

"No," she said, "we'll let Barry carry it, because when he comes back, I might stay in Leadville a day or two, to see Horace."

"Okay," Jensen said. "I'll talk to Barry after breakfast, and then the two of you can saddle up."

They all looked down the table to where Windham was sitting. Although he looked nervous it didn't seem to have affected his appetite, as he shoveled flapjacks into his mouth.

After breakfast, as the miners filed out, Jensen, Riley and Roxy remained in their seats, as did Windham, who had been instructed to do so the night before.

Roxy stood up and walked down to where the messenger was seated.

"It's you and me, Barry," she said.

"Huh?"

"We've decided that you and I will go ahead and start riding to Leadville."

"But . . . what if somebody tries to kill us?"

"That's the point," she said.

"You want somebody to try and kill us?" he said, aghast.

"Yes," Roxy said, "so I can catch them and find out who put them up to it."

"Can you catch 'em before they kill us?" he asked.

She put her hand on his thin shoulder and said, "Let's hope so."

"Jesus," he said, swallowing hard. He looked like he might not keep his flapjacks down, but in the end, he managed.

"While we're out there," she said, "we'll also be looking for any sign of Donnie. That should make you happy."

"If we manage to find him, yeah," he said, "and as long as we stay alive."

"I'm going to do my best to make sure we stay that way," she promised.

***

When they left the mess, Roxy took Windham to the leanto so they could saddle their horses. She was actually hoping somebody might take a shot at them before they even left camp, but it didn't look like that was going to happen. When the horses were saddled, they rode them around to the front of the office.

Both Jensen and Riley stepped out of the office.

"Try not to get killed, kid," Riley called to Barry Windham.

"Aw, Jeez," Windham muttered, "why'd he have to say that?"

"Relax," Roxy said, "he's just playing it up."

"Good luck, Roxy," Riley called.

Roxy waved, and she and Windham rode off. She was aware that there were a lot of eyes following their progress. Hopefully, one set belonged to the man she wanted.

***

As Roxy and Windham got clear of the camp, the young man began to fidget in the saddle, his head swiveling around so much she thought he'd for sure sprained his neck.

"Settle down," she said. "Even if someone is going to take a shot at us, they're going to wait until we're far enough away from the camp so nobody there hears it."

"Sorry, sorry," Windham said, "I'm just . . . I ain't never been shot at before."

"And you might not now," she told him. "Let's just see what happens."

"Do you think we might find Donnie?"

She thought it was more likely they'd find the other messenger's body, but she said, "Could be. If we do, he's going to need a lot of help."

"Maybe he'll be able to tell us who shot him," he said, hopefully.

"Yeah, maybe," Roxy replied.

At least Windham was starting to sound a little more positive.

As they got further away from the mining camp, Roxy became more aware of her surroundings. There were plenty of places somebody with a rifle could hide.

They rode single file, with Roxy taking up the rear. That way Windham couldn't see that she was now the one with her head swiveling about on her neck. She was watching for movement, reflections, or hoping to catch just a glimpse of somebody in the rocks around them.

She hated the idea that they might have a watcher or watchers that she was not aware of.

Chapter Thirty-Six

Roxy called out to Windham to stop.

"What is it?" he asked.

"We're about halfway," she said. "Let's rest the horses."

They dismounted, allowed the horses to drink from a nearby stream, had their own fill and then replenished their canteens.

"What if we get to Leadville without anyone takin' a shot at us?" Windham asked.

"Then our plan didn't work," she said, "but at least we'll deliver our message to Horace Tabor."

"So then we'll be successful."

"In one way, yes," she said.

"And then Mr. Tabor will send guards to the mine, and it'll become like a prison."

"You're looking at it the wrong way."

"Am I?" he asked. "They'll have guns, and there'll be rules—"

"Aren't there rules now?"

"Only one," he said. "Everybody does their job."

"Everybody who lives, you mean," she said. "Come on, let's keep moving."

They mounted their horses and headed toward Leadville. Then, just at that moment, she saw the glint of sunlight reflected off . . . something.

"Down!" she shouted.

Windham hit the ground just as there was the crack of a shot. A bullet struck a rock and ricocheted away.

Roxy took cover and watched helplessly as their horses ran off.

"What are we gonna do without horses?" Windham asked, from hiding.

"First we have to get out of this alive," she said, "and then we walk."

There was another shot, and ricochet.

"Where is he?" Windham asked.

"Up there," she said, pointing above them.

"Where? I don't see him. Or them."

"Just one shooter," she said. "With a rifle."

"And our rifles are on our horses," he said.

"Then" she said, "we'll just have to get closer."

"How do we do that?"

"Very carefully."

***

Roxy told Windham to follow her, and then started moving from rock to rock, waiting to draw another shot.

Only it didn't come. Finally, she reached the point where she thought the shooter was operating from.

"See? Scuff marks on the rocks," she said, pointing.

"Then where did he go?" Windham asked.

"He took two shots and missed," she said. "He's going to find a new hiding place and try again."

"And what do we do?"

"We find him."

"How?"

"I'll track him," she said.

"Are you a good tracker?"

"Good enough for this," she said. "He drags his feet, see? Heel marks."

"Why doesn't he have a horse?" he asked, as she started walking.

"He probably does, and he's going to it now. Let's hurry it up so we can see if we can catch up."

As she increased the pace, she became aware of Windham's labored breathing. When she tuned to look, he had lagged far behind.

"Go," he gasped, waving, "go, I'll catch up."

If she left him behind, the shooter might circle around and kill him. On the other hand, if she waited for him, the shooter might get away.

"Keep a sharp eye out!" she warned.

He nodded, waved and she moved on ahead.

She had the feeling she was catching up, and then noticed something. She bent down to examine it further, but felt sure she was looking at drops of dry blood. Was the shooter injured? Had Donnie Evans given as good as he'd gotten?

She continued to find the trail of scuff marks. She turned several times to see where Windham was, but he was now so far behind that he was out of sight. She felt sure she would have heard any more shots. She just hoped no one had gotten closer to the young man and stuck a knife in him. If that was the case, she was going to feel really terrible for leaving him behind.

But she couldn't worry about that now. She had to keep moving. It was getting on toward dusk, and she didn't want to be wandering around these rocks in the dark. They were no longer on the mountain, but in the foothills beneath it. Still, there were plenty of ways to get hurt in the dark.

***

Ahead of her—but not that far ahead—the man with the rifle was cursing his footing in these hills as he made his way back to his horse. He was upset with himself that he'd missed—twice. His foot was still aching and, sometimes, bleeding, and he needed to get into Leadville to see a doctor, but he couldn't do that until the job was finished.

And the job was to kill Lady Gunsmith.

***

Roxy spotted more blood, fresher, this time, as if whatever wound the man had was bleeding, again. She decided to pick up the pace, rocks or no rocks.

Within minutes she saw a man up ahead, carrying a rifle, limping through the rocks.

"Hold it, there" she shouted.

The man turned and brought the rifle up without hesitation. She had no choice but to draw and fire. The rifle went flying from his hands as he fell over backwards.

She picked her way through the rocks until she reached him, looked down and was only mildly surprised to see that the dead man—the man who had taken the shot at them—was Donnie Evans.

Chapter Thirty-Seven

Roxy leaned over Evans' body and checked to make sure he was dead. Then she looked at his right foot, which was bleeding through his boot. She assumed he had injured himself at some point during his "ride" to Leadville—maybe fell off his horse and nicked it on a sharp rock—then put the blood on his saddle and sent his horse home.

So Evans was one of the saboteurs. It was too bad she couldn't have taken him alive, to find out who he was working for. She couldn't accept that Donnie Evans was the brains.

She turned to look behind her, still waiting for the other messenger, Barry Windham, to catch up, but there was no sign of him.

After searching Evans' pockets and coming up with nothing, she left the body to rot in the sun. She couldn't have buried it even if she wanted to. The ground was solid rock.

What she needed to do now was find their horses. As she turned away from Evans' body, there was the crack of another shot. A bullet struck the ground in front of her, sending sparks flying, a bit of stone cut into her leg.

She dove for cover, banging her knee hard as she did. Gun in hand, she scanned the distance to see where the shot had come from. She knew she had been extremely lucky to have three shots miss. She couldn't count on a fourth. Yet she had to find out who was shooting at her, now that Evans was dead.

She looked down at Evans again, decided to pick up his rifle and holster her pistol. Now if she spotted the shooter in the distance, she could take a shot. But was he still out there? Maybe he'd taken one last shot at her, and gone looking for horses, himself.

She stood up, ran forward several yards, and then sought cover again. There was no shot. If there were two shooters, why wouldn't they both have tried at the same time? Why would one wait 'til the other was dead?

She thought about Barry Windham. Either he was stumbling around out there, or he was the second shooter. If that was true, then he and Evans both fooled everyone, including her. The only way to find out for sure was to find Windham.

She stood again, ran a few yards, and ducked down. Still no shot.

She stood up slowly, moved forward, keeping alert, but there were no further shots. She decided to make her way back to where she last saw Windham, and the horses. Then she realized she should have gone the other way.

Evans was bound to have a horse secreted somewhere. If she didn't find hers, she would have to come back.

Finally, she saw Windham. She recognized him from the back, as he was tall and gangly. Then she wondered why she was seeing his back? He was supposed to be coming after her. Also, he was carrying a rifle, which he hadn't had the last time she saw him. Why had he turned to go the other way? Maybe because he had taken that last shot, and missed?

As she got closer, she called out, "Barry!"

He turned, saw her, and then started running. Obviously, he wanted to get away from her.

She raised the rifle she borrowed from the dead man and fired two shots, one to his left and one to his right, each sending up a shower of sparks as they ricocheted off the stones.

Windham stopped short and put his hands in the air.

As she closed the distance and caught up to him, she said, "Drop the rifle."

He did so, in a spasmatic move, tossing it aside.

"What the hell's going on, Barry?" she said. "I found Donnie."

"Is he dead?"

"He is now," she said. "He was alive enough to shoot at us. Or was he just shooting at me?"

"Look," he said, "I didn't want nothin' to do with this, but Donnie said we'd get a lot of money—enough to get us outta that minin' camp."

"And all you had to do was what?"

"Get you out here," he said.

"Where Donnie could kill me?"

"Well . . ."

"Where you were both supposed to kill me?"

"I didn't wanna do it!" he said, quickly. "But—"

"But Donnie said there'd be a lot of money in it," Roxy said. "So after he missed and I went after him, you took a shot at me."

"Um, sorta—"

"Sort of?"

"Yeah, kinda—look, if you killed him, then I'm done. You can just let me go."

"I don't think so, Barry."

"Why not?"

"Because you're going to tell me who you and Evans were working for."

"I don't know that!" he said. "Honest. Donnie was the one."

"That's real convenient, saying dead Donnie's the one who knew who you were working for."

"It's the truth! Honest!" he blurted. "Can I put my hands down, now?"

"Not yet. We're not done."

Roxy's leg was throbbing.

"Where'd you get the rifle?"

"From my horse."

"You know where the horses are?"

"Yeah, they didn't go far," he said. "They came wanderin' back, so I grabbed my rifle."

"And my horse?"

"Yeah, it came back, too."

"How far are they?" she asked.

"Not too far," he said. "I was headed there. I rounded their reins and put a rock on top. They ain't goin' nowhere."

"Take me to them, Barry," she said, "and they better be there."

"They are."

"Let's move."

"W-what about my rifle?"

"You're not going to need it," she said. "Start walking."

Chapter Thirty-Eight

They walked about a mile before she saw the horses standing quietly.

"Mount up, Barry," she said.

"Can we rest here a minute?" he asked.

"Rest in the saddle."

"Are you lettin' me go?" he asked, hopefully. "Now that you got your horse?"

"No, Barry," she said. "I'm not letting you go. We're heading for Leadville."

"Why there?" he asked. "Why don't we go back to camp?"

"Because we're closer to Leadville," she said. "And that's where Horace Tabor is."

"Mr. Tabor?"

"Yes," she said, "he wants to know who was sabotaging his operation. I'm going to tell him it was you and Donnie, and Donnie's dead."

"But . . . ya can't blame it all on me," Windham said. "He'll kill me."

"Probably," she said, "but he paid me to do a job, and I'm going to do it."

"B-but I'm nobody," he said. "I ain't behind the whole thing."

"I know, but you said Donnie was the only one who knew who was," Roxy said. "And I can't very well turn him over to Mr. Tabor, can I? Because he's dead, already."

"Aw. Roxy—"

"Miss Doyle will do, Barry," she said. "Now mount up."

He reluctantly climbed into the saddle, and then she saw him tense.

"You try to run, and I'll shoot you right out of the saddle, Barry."

"Aw, look—"

"What?"

"What if I did have a name?"

"But you said you didn't," Roxy said.

"But what if I did?"

"Then it would probably do you a lot of good to give that name to Mr. Tabor."

"I could give it to you, and you could give it to him and let me go."

"And what if you were lying to me, Barry?"

"But I wouldn't—"

"Because you don't lie, right?"

She mounted her own horse, tossed away Evans' rifle because she now had her own.

"Let's go, Barry," she said. "You'll ride ahead of me."

"You're too young to be so scary, Miss," he said.

"I'm older than you, Barry," she said. "A lot older, and much more experienced."

***

When they reached Leadville, Roxy picked out a very unassuming little hotel on a side street, rather than go back to Horace Tabor's Grand Hotel. Down the street was a livery stable where they left their horses.

She checked in, winked at the desk clerk, and took Windham up to the room.

"Now what?" Windham asked, when they were locked inside.

"I've been thinking," she said. "I think I believe Gus Jensen when he said none of the men at the mine are involved in the, uh, accidents."

"But Donnie and me—"

"Yes, I know," she said, "you work at the mine, but not *in* the mine. Gus said none of the miners would be involved. They don't benefit from it. But somebody does."

"Who?"

"That's something I'm going to guess about," she said.

"So you think Donnie was hired—uh, we were hired—by somebody here in Leadville?"

"Or Denver," she said. "But you said you were going to give Mr. Tabor a name."

"Well, uh, it's just a name I heard Donnie say once."

"That should be enough," Roxy said. "If Mr. Tabor recognizes the name, we'll be in business."

"Business?"

"We'll know who to go after."

"And then you'll let me go?"

"That'll be up to Mr. Tabor," she said. She walked to the dresser and looked in the pitcher.

"I'm going to get cleaned up," she said, pouring some water into the basin, "and then you can do the same."

"And can we get somethin' to eat?" he asked.

As she washed her hands she said, "You took a shot at me, and you want me to feed you?"

"I'm a terrible shot," he assured her.

She laughed, dried her hands on a nearby towel, and said, "Okay, sure, we'll get something to eat. And then we'll go and see Mr. Tabor. But first you wash up."

"Oh, yeah, sure."

He got up and went to the dresser and used the same water to wash his hands.

Roxy walked to the window and looked out. It overlooked the main street, but there was no access, and there wasn't a building across the street of comparable height, from where somebody might take a shot at her. She looked down at the street, which was not well traveled.

"All done."

She turned and saw Windham drying his hands, leaving dirty tracks on the towel.

"Good," she said. "Let's get that meal." She waved at the door. "You first, and remember what I said about running."

"I know," Windham said. "You'll shoot me."

Chapter Thirty-Nine

They stopped in a small café that wasn't doing a brisk business. Roxy was able to get a table in the back, sat Windham with his back to the door. They both had the special, which was beef stew.

"You ain't had second thoughts, have you?" he asked, as they finished.

"About what?"

"About takin' me to see Mr. Tabor?"

"No," she said, "no second thoughts about that."

"He might kill me, you know," Windham said. "And I mean, on the spot."

"And it's because of you and your friend Donnie that I had to kill a man, remember?"

"B-but . . . it was Donnie you killed."

"Which, once again, leaves only you. I hope that name you've got does you some good."

"So do I," Windham said.

"Why don't we go and see?"

***

Roxy paid the bill and they left the restaurant. She wasn't sure whether to go to Tabor's house, or to the

Grand Hotel. Finally, she decided on the hotel. She might find Tabor's man, Grant, there, or Baby Doe. One of them could tell her where Horace Tabor was.

As they entered the cavernous lobby Barry Windham's eyes went wide, and he almost walked into people several times as he was studying the ceiling.

"Ah, Miss Doyle," the desk clerk said, smiling. "Welcome back. Same room?"

"Not right now, thanks," she said. "Is Mr. Tabor in?"

"I'm sorry, he's not," the clerk said. "He went out early this morning."

"Do you know if he's at his house?"

"I couldn't say," the clerk replied.

"Do you know if Mrs. Tabor is in her suite?"

"Oh, yes, Baby Doe's there." He covered his mouth with his hands quickly. "Oh, geez, you won't tell her I called her that, will you?"

"It'll be our secret," she said. "I'm going up and see her."

"That's fine, Miss."

"I'm leaving this man here in the lobby," she said. "If he tries to leave, shoot him. If you let him leave, I'll shoot you. Understand?"

"Perfectly, Miss," the clerk said.

She looked at Windham.

"Yeah, yeah, I understand."

There was an elevator that she had not used last time she was there, and she ignored it this time, as well. She took the stairs to the third floor and knocked on Baby Doe's door.

"Well," Elizabeth Tabor said, when she saw Roxy standing in the hall, "nice to see you again. Come in."

"I just need a minute—"

"We're not going to have that minute in the hall," Baby Doe said. She was wearing a silk dressing gown, with fur around the neck.

Roxy entered the room and Baby Doe closed the door. The woman's make-up and hair was perfection; she was beautiful.

"Drink?" she asked.

"Too early."

"For some people," Baby Doe said. She walked across the room to a sidebar and picked up a drink she had obviously already been working on.

"What can I do for you, Roxy?"

"I'm looking for Horace."

"Are you just back from the Matchless?"

"Yes."

"How's that handsome Gus Jensen doing?" Baby Doe asked.

"There's more to a man than just looks," Roxy said.

"Ooh," Baby Doe said, "something happened between you two."

"He didn't like some of the conclusions I was coming to," Roxy said.

"That's too bad," Elizabeth said. "Why do you want Horace? Do you have the answers to his questions?"

"I have some answers," Roxy replied, "but also have more questions."

"Oh, well," she said, "Horace is not going to like that."

"I think we may come up with the answers we've been looking for," Roxy went on. "One of the men involved is already dead."

Baby Doe looked surprised at that.

"Oh! Well, Horace will love that."

"Where is he?" Roxy asked.

"At business meetings all day," Baby Doe said, "but he'll be back here tonight for supper. Can you wait until then?"

"I suppose so," Roxy said. "How about Mr. Grant?"

"George?" She looked puzzled. "What do you want with him?"

"I think he can answer some of my questions," Roxy said.

"Well, George is with Horace right now, seeing to his every wish," she said. "Perhaps he'll be back here at the hotel with him tonight."

"All right, then," Roxy said. "I'll be back this evening."

"Come at five," Baby Doe said. "We'll be getting ready for supper."

"I'll be here."

Baby Doe walked to the door with Roxy.

"It sounds to me like you might have solved Horace's problems," Elizabeth Tabor said.

"Not all of them," Roxy said, "but maybe some."

"Well, just make sure he pays you well enough for what you've done."

"I'll do my best," Roxy said, and left.

Chapter Forty

When Roxy got back to the lobby, she didn't see Windham immediately, but then saw him sitting on one of the divans. The desk clerk exchanged a nod with her as she went by.

"There you are," Windham said. "People are lookin' at me like I don't belong here."

"You don't," Roxy said. "Neither do I. Come on."

She headed for the door, and he hurriedly followed.

"Where are we headed?" he asked. "Are we gonna see Mr. Tabor?"

"Later this evening," she said.

When they got outside the Grand Hotel, Roxy stopped for a moment.

"Where are we headed?" Windham asked, anxiously.

"I'm not sure."

"You're not sure?" he asked. "I thought you had this all figured out."

"I don't have anything figured out, except that you and Evans turned on your employers," Roxy pointed out. "In fact, you turned on your fellow employees, too."

"Look, I never meant to hurt nobody—"

"Except for some dead miners and, oh yeah," she added, "me!"

"Look, Miss Doyle—"

"Just keep quiet, Barry," she said. "Don't make me wish I had shot you instead of your partner."

The sound his mouth made as he snapped it shut was audible.

***

George Grant read the message that had just been delivered to him by a runner. He was in the lobby of the Tabor Opera House, in Leadville, where Horace Tabor was having a business meeting with several colleagues/rivals. It had been sent by Elizabeth Tabor, and was informing her husband that Roxy Doyle was back in Leadville, and apparently had some answers for him about who had been sabotaging his Matchless Mine.

Grant knew Tabor would want to see this message as soon as possible, but he had been warned not to interrupt his boss during business meetings. So he folded the message, stuck it in his pocket, and waited.

***

There wasn't much for Roxy to do in Leadville to kill time. She could have a drink in a saloon, or do some gambling, but neither of those things would go well with

Barry Windham cramping her style. So she simply took them back to their hole-in-the-wall hotel, locked the young man in his room and took the key. If he wanted to jump out the window, it was high enough for a broken leg to be the result.

She sat in her own room, wondering if she could sneak out to a saloon for a drink without any adverse consequences, but decided not to risk it. She kicked off her boots, reclined on the bed, and proceeded to get the sleep she had been missing for days.

***

Horace Tabor came walking across the opera house lobby toward George Grant, looking satisfied with himself.

"Did it go the way you wanted it to, sir?" Grant asked.

"Exactly the way I wanted, Grant," Tabor said. "And what have you been doing while I've been working, huh? Drinking in the bar?"

"No, sir," Grant said. "I was sitting right here, waiting for you."

"How boring for you."

"Well, not really," Grant said. He considered not giving Tabor the message, but then Baby Doe was sure to tell him she sent it, and he'd have to explain. Saying he had forgotten would just not sit right. “A messenger came with a note for you.”

“Eh? Well, where is it?”

“Here.” Grant took it from his pocket and handed it to his boss.

Tabor unfolded the message and read it.

“Why didn’t you come in and give it to me?” he asked.

“You, uh, said you didn’t want to be disturbed.”

“Unless it was for something important,” Tabor said. “This is important. Come on, let’s see what she’s found out.”

“In the message Mrs. Tabor said that Miss Doyle would be back while you were dressing for dinner,” Grant said.

“Let’s get back to the hotel,” Horace said. “Maybe we can catch her before that.”

Grant watched as his boss shoved the message into his pocket, and then they were rushing to the door.

***

Roxy was antsy.

She was worried that Windham might have taken a chance on the broken leg and lit out, deciding to risk his life to get away, so she walked down the hall to his room and knocked. After a moment she was about to knock again when the door opened and he stood there, bleary eyed . . . and naked.

"I was sleepin'," he said.

"I can see that."

She could see a lot more. He was tall and skinny, but between his legs was a beautiful specimen of the male penis, semi-hard from whatever dream she had awakened him from.

He saw her looking at him and suddenly got shy. He tried to cover his crotch with his hands, but she pushed them away.

"Relax," she said, putting her hand against his skinny chest. "Back up."

"Why?"

"So I can close the door and come in."

He obeyed, and when she was inside, she looked down at him again.

"I better get dressed—"

"I said relax," she told him. "We're not going anywhere, yet."

"Well . . . I'm naked," he said, "and we both know you're a slut." He reached down, began to stoke himself. "I got what you want right here, don't I? Come on, see how big? You want it, right?"

"Well . . ."

She reached out, grasped his penis in one hand, and began to stroke it.

Chapter Forty-One

"Oh God!" he gasped, as she stroked him to fullness.

She sat back on her heels and stared at it.

"Wow, that's a long one," she said. "You get much use out of it?"

"Uh . . . a whore, sometimes."

"Too bad."

As she stared at it, it seemed to continue to grow.

She leaned forward again, took it in her hand and pumped it a few times.

"Jesus!" he said, and flopped down on his back.

Then she tightened her hold and began to squeeze.

"Hey, ow!" he said. "What're ya—"

"You think you're in charge here, Barry?" she asked, squeezing even tighter.

"Owww!"

"You're not in charge," she went on, "and you never will be. Got it?"

"Yeah, yeah, ow, I got it, leggo!"

Instead of letting go, she reached with her other hand, grabbed his balls and squeezed them.

"Owwwwww," he howled.

"I tell you what," she said. "You answer some questions and I'll let go."

"Anything," he said, desperate now.

"Did you and Donnie have a plan all along? When he rode out?"

"Huh? Oh, yeah, yeah . . . Ooh, Jesus."

"What was the plan?"

"I went out and hid a horse that we kept nearby. He was gonna ride out, and switch horses so his would come back without him. He thought you'd go out lookin' for him, and then he could shoot you."

"And you'd go with me?"

"If I could," he said. "I, uh, I didn't know it'd be your idea."

"Do you know why there was blood on the saddle?"

"No," he said, "I, uh, oooh, Geez . . . I guess he thought it'd look good."

"His foot was hurt," she said. "I think maybe it was a lucky accident, and he made use of it."

"Yeah, yeah, Donnie was smart . . . oh God . . ."

"One more question, Barry."

"Yeah, yah, anything, just . . . yeah . . ."

"The name of the man," she said.

"Name? What name?"

"You said Donnie mentioned a name."

"Oh, yeah, he did."

"What was it?" She started to pump his cock faster. It turned almost purple.

"Oh God," he gasped, "holy . . . uh, uh, it was . . . Hec, he said the name Hec."

"Hec?" She frowned. "Are you sure? That's all?" She squeezed.

"Yeah, yeah, that was it. Just . . . Hec . . . Jesus!"

She released her hold on him and stood up.

"Very impressive cock, Barry."

He stared up at her, his eyes glassy.

"Um, I thought you were gonna— that you might—"

"What?" she asked. "Suck it? Sit on it? Sorry, Barry, it's nice, but we're going to be a little busy. Besides, you need a bath." She reached down and slapped it, making him jump. "Get dressed. It's almost supper time. Come down the hall to my room when you're . . . clean."

She went out the door and back down the hall to her own room so she could wash her hands.

***

Horace Tabor entered the lobby of the Grand Hotel with George Grant trotting after him. He went right to the desk clerk.

"Oh, hello, Mr. Tabor, sir," the clerk said.

"Is Roxy Doyle in her room?"

"No, sir."

"But she was here earlier in the day?"

"Yes, sir," the clerk said, nervously. "She said she didn't need the room."

"What did she do when she was here?"

"She, uh, went up to see your wife, sir."

"And is my wife up there now?"

"Yessir."

With a short nod Horace Tabor headed for the elevator, Grant right behind him. The clerk breathed a sigh of relief. He had heard stories of employees being fired because Horace Tabor wasn't happy. For now, he still had a job.

***

Baby Doe opened the door to her room, expecting to see Roxy Doyle.

"Horace!" she said, surprised. "Why didn't you use your key?"

"Grant's with me," he said. "I wanted to warn you, in case . . ."

"I was naked? As you can see," she said, "I'm dressed, but why don't you have him wait downstairs, anyway?"

Grant, who was standing off to one side, heard her and said, “I can do that, sir.”

“Then do it,” Horace said. “And if Roxy Dole comes in, bring her up.”

“Yes sir.”

Tabor stepped into the room and closed the door. He turned, looked at his wife in her blue dress, her hair pinned up on her head to reveal her long, graceful neck.

“You look lovely, my dear,” he said, “as usual.”

“We’re going out to supper, after all,” she said.

“Yes,” he said, “but first—”

“How did your business go today?”

“Perfectly,” he said. “I got everything I wanted.”

“Don’t you always?”

“I don’t know,” he said. “That’s what I was going to ask you. I got your message. What did Miss Doyle have to say?”

“Nothing, to me,” Baby Doe replied. “Whatever she has to say she feels compelled to tell you. After all, you hired her.”

“Yes,” he said, “but did she give you a clue?”

“She said one man was dead.”

“That’s all?”

Baby Doe arched an eyebrow.

“You wanted her to kill more?”

“No, I mean, that’s all she said?”

"Yes," Baby Doe said, "but I told her to come back here before we go to supper, so she should be—" She looked at the clock on top of a nearby cabinet—"any minute actually. She should arrive while you're changing for supper."

"Yes," he said, removing his jacket, "of course."

He headed for the bedroom.

"The grey suit, I think," Elizabeth called after him.

***

When Roxy and Windham entered the Grand Hotel lobby again, she saw George Grant sitting on a divan. She changed direction and walked over to him.

"George," she said.

He either hadn't seen her enter, or he was simply pretending not to.

"Oh, Miss Doyle." He stood up. "How very nice it is to see you again."

"Is the boss upstairs?" she asked.

"Yes, he's getting dressed for supper."

"I should go up there, then," she said. "Oh, I'm sorry. Do you two know each other?"

"Huh?" Windham said, nervously. "Uh, no, but I've heard the name."

“Yes,” Grant said, “and I’ve heard Mr. Windham’s name. He’s one of the messengers from the mine, right?”

“That’s right. I better go up.”

“I can wait down here,” Windham offered. He and Grant seemed to be trying not to look at each other.

“No, Barry, you better come upstairs with me to see Mr. Tabor,” she said.

“Uh, yeah, okay,” Windham said, tearing his gaze away from Grant.

“I’ll just continue to wait right here,” Grant said, and sat back down.

“You do that, Mr. Grant,” Roxy said. “I’m sure Horace and Baby Doe will be down soon to go to supper. Will you be joining them?”

“I doubt it,” Grant said. “They prefer to eat alone.”

Chapter Forty-Two

Roxy knocked and the door was opened by Baby Doe.

"Hi, Roxy," she said. "Come on in. Horace is getting dressed. He'll be out in a minute."

Roxy entered and closed the door. She looked at Elizabeth Tabor in her long blue dress and upswept hair, and knew why they said she was the most beautiful woman in Denver.

"Would you like a drink while we wait?" Baby Doe asked.

"No, thanks. I saw Mr. Grant downstairs."

"Yes, he's waiting around to do my husband's bidding."

"Will he go to supper with you?"

"Oh, no," she said. "Horace likes for us to eat alone, just the two of us. Although I'm sure he'd be glad for you to join us."

"I don't think so," Roxy said. "I just want to talk to him—" She stopped short when Tabor entered from the other room.

"Miss Doyle," he said, "how nice." He was impeccably dressed in an expensive grey suit. "I assume you have some news for me? I heard you killed one of the saboteurs."

"Yes, his name was Donnie Evans."

"Evans." Tabor frowned. "Wait, he delivered a couple of messages to me."

"That's right," she said. "He was used as a messenger."

"But . . . he couldn't be the head man. Surely he was working for someone."

"I'm sure he was."

"And you don't know who?"

"No, he didn't leave me much. I had to kill him before he could talk."

"So how do you intend to find out who he was working for?" Tabor asked.

"There's another man, another messenger," Roxy said. "They were working together."

"That's great!" Tabor said. "Where is he?"

"Out in the hall."

"Alone?" Tabor snapped. "You left him alone? What makes you think he'll still be there?"

"He'll be there."

"Well, then, get him in here," Tabor said. "I want to hear that name."

It suddenly occurred to Roxy where she had heard the name before. If she was right . . .

"You may not like what you hear, Horace," she said.

"Never mind that," he said. "I want to hear it."

"Now take it easy, dear," Elizabeth said, putting her hand on her husband's arm. "Don't snap at Roxy."

"Sorry, sorry," Tabor said, "you're right, of course." He covered her hand with his and looked at Roxy. "Please bring him in, Roxy, and let's hear what he has to say."

Roxy walked to the door.

Chapter Forty-Three

When she stuck her head out the door, Barry Windham looked at her hopefully. Maybe he thought they'd fuck after this, poor sap.

"Come on in, Barry," she said. "Mr. Tabor wants to see you."

She backed away and allowed the young man to enter.

"Mr. Tabor, this is Barry Windham," she said.

"Mr. Tabor—"

"How long have you worked for me, Windham?" Tabor asked, cutting him off.

"A few months, sir."

"And that's how long you and your friend have been causing accidents at my mine?"

"It wasn't nothin' personal, sir," Windham said. "Just a way to make money."

"I wasn't paying you enough?"

"It was Donnie," he said. "I mean, his idea to get us a lot of money, fast."

"But you worked for somebody."

"Uh, yeah, but Donnie knew him, not me."

Tabor looked at Roxy.

"You said he knew a name."

"He told me he heard his friend Donnie say a name once," she replied. "Go ahead, Barry. Tell him."

Windham looked at Tabor.

"Tell me."

"And then you'll have her kill me," Windham said.

"If you tell me who you were working for," Tabor said, "you can walk out of here."

Windham looked at Roxy.

"Does he mean it?"

"My husband doesn't lie," Baby Doe said.

Windham looked at Tabor.

"I once asked Donnie how much we would be gettin'," Windham said. "And he told me . . . Hec was gonna pay us a bundle."

"Hec?"

"That's what he said."

Tabor thought about it for a few moments, then said to Windham, "Get out."

"Can I have some money?" the young man asked.

"Don't push it!" Tabor said. He looked at Roxy. "Get him out of here."

"Come on," Roxy said, and opened the door.

"Will I see you again?" Windham asked, as he passed her.

"You better hope not."

Windham looked disappointed and stepped into the hall. Then he turned back.

"Is there a back way out?"

"Why?" she asked. "Don't you want to see George Grant on your way out?"

"Well, uh—"

"You know him, don't you?"

"Um . . ."

"If you wait," Roxy said, "and work with me, I'll get you some money."

He brightened.

"I'll wait!"

She closed the door, turned back to Horace Tabor, who was huddled with Baby Doe.

"Hec is your man in Denver, isn't he?" she asked. "Hector?"

"Hector Kane," Tabor said.

"Your Denver gopher. Maybe you should give your people better titles."

"I'll have his head when I get back to Denver."

"What about Grant?"

"George?" Tabor asked. "What about him?"

"He's a gopher too, isn't he?"

"You think Hector and George are working together?" Tabor asked.

"Windham recognized Grant downstairs," she said. "And grant knew him. How else?"

"Am I surrounded by turncoats?" he asked.

"Not me, dear," Baby Doe said.

"And not your men at the Matchless Mine," Roxy said. "I believe that."

"Will you continue to help me?" Tabor asked.

"I will," Roxy said, "until the end."

"So what do we do?" Tabor asked. "How do we learn why these two became traitors?"

"I have an idea . . ."

***

When Roxy came out of the room, Windham was leaning against the wall.

"Where are we goin'?" he asked. His eyes suddenly resembled those of a puppy.

"First," she said, "you know Grant, don't you?"

"I don't know this Hec Donnie talked about," Windham said, "but I do know George Grant."

"How?"

"I delivered a message to him one time."

"And?"

"And he gave me a message to deliver to Donnie."

"Ah."

"So who's this Hec?" Windham asked.

"Hector Kane," Roxy said, "he does in Denver what George Grant does here in Leadville."

"So they're workin' together."

"Obviously," Roxy said. "What we don't know is why they decided to try and shut down the Matchless Mine."

"How are you gonna find out?" the young man asked.

"The only way I can," she said. "I'm going to ask them."

Chapter Forty-Four

When Roxy and Windham got to the lobby, George Grant was gone. However, just at that moment the desk clerk came running in from outside.

"Miss Doyle," he said, "I'm glad you're here."

"What's wrong?"

"After you went upstairs, Mr. Grant hurried out, and I followed him."

"Why did you do that?"

He shrugged.

"I just thought you and Mr. Tabor might like me to do it," he explained.

"Actually, we are glad," Roxy said. "Where did he go?"

"Just down the street to the telegraph office," the clerk said.

"Is he still there?"

"He was when I left to come back here and tell you," the young man said. "You want me to run back and check?"

"No, that's okay," she said. "You've done enough. You better get back to work. Your boss will be down, soon."

"Yes, Miss."

He hurried to get around behind the desk before Tabor came down.

"Whatawe do now?" Windham asked.

"Let's go and see what this telegram is all about," Roxy said.

***

When they got to the telegraph office, there was no sign of Grant. It was getting late, stores around them were closed or closing, but the chubby telegraph clerk was still seated behind the desk. When he saw Roxy enter, he got to his feet quickly, sucking in his gut.

"Can I help ya?" he asked.

"Yes, a man was just in here sending a telegram, maybe you know him? George Grant?"

"Oh yeah, Mr. Grant works for Mr. Tabor."

"Right," Roxy sad. "I need to know where he sent a telegram to."

"Um," the young clerk said, frowning, "I ain't supposed to give that kind of information out."

"Look," Roxy said, "Mr. Tabor sent me over here to find out. Now, if I have to go back and tell him he has to come here himself—"

"No, no," the clerk said, "you don't gotta do that. Just hold on."

He turned, leafed through a stack of papers, then turned back, holding one.

“He sent it to Denver.”

“To who?”

“Fella named Hector Kane.”

“What’s it say?” Roxy asked.

“It just says ‘Get here fast, we got trouble.’”

“There,” Roxy said, “that wasn’t so hard, was it?”

“No, Ma’am.”

She gave him a dollar and said, “Thank you.” It was one of her last silver dollars, but Tabor was supposed to be paying her a bundle for this.

“Come on,” she said to Windham, and they left.

“So this Hec’s comin’ here?” he asked, as they got outside.

“Looks like it,” she said.

“To do what?”

“I don’t know,” she said. “Do you know of any other men working for Hec? Did Donnie mention anyone else?”

“Well,” Windham said, “there’s gotta be somebody else.”

“Why’s that?”

“Because me and Donnie, we didn’t kill nobody.”

“What? You didn’t kill the Pinkertons?”

"No, Ma'am," he said. "That's why I wasn't so happy when Donnie said we was gonna kill you. That ain't what we do."

"Well, that's just fine," Roxy said. "That means there's probably still a killer or two up at the mine. You should've told me this before, Barry."

"Geez, Roxy," he said, "you never asked me."

***

Roxy wasn't going to interrupt the Tabor's private supper. Besides, she didn't know where they were eating. So she decided to get something to eat herself before going back to the Grand Hotel to talk to the Tabors.

"Where are we goin' now?" Windham asked.

"Mr. Tabor said you could go," she told him.

"Go where? I can't go back to camp, and I have no money."

"All right," she said. "Come with me. I know where we can eat for free."

She took him to the Grand Hotel dining room, where she still had Tabor paying her bill.

They both had steak dinners, during which an idea occurred to Roxy.

"You said you can't go back to the camp," she said, "but nobody there knows what's happened. As far as they know, you still work there."

"What's your point?"

"You know where to find Grant, don't you?" she asked. "I mean, if you had a message for him?"

Windham hesitated, then said, "Yes, but I don't want to work for him anymore."

"Maybe," she said, "you only need to do one more job."

***

After supper, Roxy told Windham she was going to go talk to the Tabors again."

"And what do I do? Wait in the hall, again?"

"No," she said, "you go and find Grant. Tell him you got away from me. Don't tell him you gave us Hec's name or admitted that you know him."

"So what do I say?"

"Nothing," she said, "because if I'm right, he'll give you a message to take back to the mine. And without Evans, he'll have to tell you exactly who to deliver it to."

"And then what do I do?"

"You bring the message to me."

"Oh, and you'll know who's really working against the mine up there."

"Right."

"And if I do this . . ."

"Yes?"

"Will you, uh, do what we did in my room," he asked, "only more?"

"Barry—"

"If you really want me to do this . . ." he said, ". . . I'll even take a bath."

"Barry, are you really trying to trade for sex?" she asked.

"Not just sex," he said, "sex with you—just once! I swear, I won't bother you again after that."

He was tall and gangly and not at all handsome, but he did have one body part she found interesting.

"All I'm going to say," she told him, "is that I'll consider it."

He thought a moment, then said, "Okay, I'll do it. But what if he doesn't give me a message?"

"Well then," she said, "I'll have to admit I was wrong."

Chapter Forty-Five

"Where's the kid?" Tabor asked, as he and Baby Doe let Roxy into their room again. Both of them had undressed and were wearing expensive looking robes. Roxy had the distinct impression that Elizabeth was naked under hers.

"You told him he could go," Roxy reminded him.

"Yes, but I didn't think you would let him go." He sat, crossed his legs, and for a split second Roxy could see that he was naked underneath, until he folded the robe over his legs.

"I sent him to see Grant."

"George? Why? Is George still in town? Why didn't you bring him—"

"Let her explain, dear," Baby Doe said.

"Yes, of course, dear."

"Go ahead, Roxy," Elizabeth said. She remained standing with a drink in her hand. "Would you like a drink first?"

"Actually," Roxy said, "Yes, I would."

Baby Doe made Roxy a drink and brought it to her. As she handed her the brandy glass their hands touched, and Baby Doe's lingered for just a moment.

"Now go ahead, my dear," Horace Tabor said.

Roxy explained that Grant had sent a telegram to Hector Kane telling him to come to Leadville right away. She also told the Tabors how she had sent Windham to Grant, hoping that the man would give the young messenger something to deliver to the mine.

"If he does," she finished, "he'll bring it here to me, and we'll have the name of the person at the mine who's working against you."

"It sounds ingenious," Baby Doe said, raising her glass. "I salute you."

Roxy also raised her glass, then drained it, and Baby Doe refilled it for her.

"I must say I'm rather nervous," Tabor admitted. "I'd hate to find out that the culprit is someone I've trusted all these months."

"My darling," Baby Doe said, "you know what you need when you get nervous."

"Yes, my love, I do."

Baby Doe put her glass down, unbelted her robe and allowed it to fall to the floor. As Roxy had suspected, she was naked beneath it. Her body almost glowed, her skin was so pale and smooth, her breasts high and firm, topped with brown nipples. Roxy could smell not only perfume in the air, but sex. She felt warm and wondered if two glasses of brandy were going to her head. She was, after all, usually a beer drinker.

Horace Tabor stood up, undid his belt and let his robe fall to the floor, as well. He was pale, though not the glowing kind of his lovely wife. He had a pot belly, and a penis that was flaccid at the moment, hanging down from the heavy gray/black bush.

He walked over to his wife, cupped one of her breasts and kissed her. She reached down to stroke his cock, which began to come to life.

"Are we making you uncomfortable, Roxy?" Baby Doe asked.

"Yes, as a matter of fact," Roxy said.

"Well then, we'll just take it into the bedroom," Elizabeth said. "Of course, you could join us, you know."

"Yes, why don't you, Roxy?" Horace Tabor asked. "It'll certainly help pass the time."

"I don't think so," she said. "Your wife is so beautiful I wouldn't want to be a disappointment."

"Oh, I doubt that could happen," Baby Doe said. "You're a gorgeous woman, Roxy, and you know it. Are you sure?"

"Positive," she said. "I think I'll go downstairs and wait for Barry to come back."

"You could wait in your room," Horace said, as they reached the door to their bedroom. Baby Doe's ass was high and rounded, while Horace's was flabby. "It's still there for you."

"I think I'll go down to the bar," Roxy said.

"Well, let me know in the morning if your plan worked," Horace said. "I'm going to want that name."

"Come on, dear," Baby Doe said, putting her hand on her husband's ass, "in you go."

"Yes, my love."

As they started away Roxy said, "Horace?"

"Yes?" They turned.

"You still owe me something."

"More money?" he asked. "You'll have it."

"No," she said, "we agreed on something else. Remember?"

"Oh, that," he said. "I'm afraid all I could find out is that you should like it in the Klondike. I'm sorry I can't be more specific."

"It's more than I had before. Thanks."

They went into the bedroom and closed the door.

Roxy put her empty glass down, decided it wasn't the brandy that had made her feel a bit dizzy and slightly ill. It was the thought of being in bed with Horace and Baby Doe Tabor.

Chapter Forty-Six

Roxy was nursing a beer at a back table when Barry Windham appeared.

"Did he do it?" she asked.

He sat across from her, grinning from ear-to-ear.

"He sure did. He was so glad when I told him I got away, that he told me right away he wanted me to take a message up to the mine."

"And did he give it to you?"

He nodded, still grinning. She knew what he was thinking.

"Don't worry, Barry," she said, "I'm still considering your offer. Where's the message?"

"Right here." He took a folded slip of paper from his pocket and slid it across the table.

She grabbed it, unfolded it and read it. It was warning the reader that there might be trouble, and maybe it was time to simply blow up the mine. What the message didn't say was who it was meant for.

"Who did he tell you to give it to?" she asked.

"Do we have a deal?" he asked.

"Yes, we have a deal," she said, impatiently. "Who was this message for?"

He told her, and at the same time she was disappointed, but not surprised.

"Can we go now?" he asked. "To your room?"

"Yes," she said. "Go up to my room and wait for me there. I just have one or two things to do."

He stood up, then asked, "Is it locked?"

"Yes," she said. "Come on."

She took him to the desk, collected her key, and gave it to him. "Now remember," she said. "Stay there and wait. Have a drink. Have two. And take a bath."

"I will!" he promised, enthusiastically. He turned and ran up the stairs.

***

Roxy knocked on the door until Horace Tabor answered it, still belting his robe.

"This better be good," he said, quite out of breath.

"I think it is."

"Come in, then."

She entered and he closed the door. When he turned to her she handed him the message.

"Is this what Grant gave the kid to deliver?" he asked.

"Yes."

He read it, and his face went pale.

"Blow the mine? That's crazy."

"Well, it's a sure way to close you down."

He stared at her.

"I just assumed whoever was behind this wanted to take the mine over, not blow it up."

"Maybe that was their plan," she said, "and now they're changing it."

He handed the message back to her.

"I want you to go back to the mine tomorrow morning and deliver this message personally," he said. "Do you understand?"

"Yes," she said, accepting it, "I do. What about Grant, and Kane, your gophers?"

"I'll have the law on them as soon as Hec arrives," Tabor said. "I'll need that messenger to talk to the sheriff."

"He's in my room in this hotel," she said. "Go easy with him. He's going to be very disappointed."

Horace looked surprised.

"Did you promise him something?"

"Yes," she said, "something I never intended to deliver, I'm afraid.

***

She spent the night in the hole-in-the-wall hotel, hoping Barry Windham had enjoyed his night at the Grand Hotel, maybe he even drank himself to sleep.

She didn't bother stopping for breakfast. Rather she bought some beef jerky from a mercantile store nearby, and ate it while she rode to the mine.

By the time she arrived later in the day, she assumed both George Grant and Hector Kane were in custody, and Horace Tabor was happy with that outcome. Now there was only her part to do.

As she rode into the camp, the men were still in the mines, and probably would be for a little less than an hour more. She rode up to the office and dismounted. She went up the steps and entered without knocking.

Gus Jensen and Stan Riley were both at the drafting table and looked up as she entered.

"Which of you knows more about dynamite?" she asked.

"I suppose that would be me," Riley said, "as the engineer."

"We wondered what happened with you and Windham. Where is he?" Jensen asked. "Did you find Evans?"

"Yes, he's dead."

"How?" Jensen asked.

"I killed him."

"You? Why?"

"Because he tried to kill me," she said. "He and Windham were working for the saboteurs."

"Did Evans tell you a name?" Riley asked.

"He didn't have time," she said, "but Windham remembered something Evans had said once, about a man named Hec."

"Hec?" Riley frowned.

"Hector Kane?" Jensen said. "Horace's man in Denver? That's who was behind all this?"

"Yes," she said, "and he had a partner."

"Who?" Jensen asked.

"George Grant."

"Oh my God," Riley said. "They're his right-hand men."

"His gophers, as he put it," she said. "I don't think they liked the title."

"Jesus," Riley said. "So . . . did you catch them?"

"Horace is taking care of that right now, with the sheriff," she said.

"Well, that's good," Jensen said. "So it's over?"

"Except for one thing," she said.

"What's that?"

Roxy walked up to Gus.

"He sent you this message."

Frowning, Gus took it, unfolded it, read it, and blanched. His eyes flicked around the room. Riley took it from the big man's limp hand and read it.

"Jesus, Gus?"

"Why, Gus?" Roxy asked.

"Horace treated me like a servant," Gus Jensen said. "The same for George and Hector. So we figured if we could put him out and take over, we'd be partners."

"And it was worth murder?" Riley asked.

"I had no choice," Jensen said. "Those Pinkertons were getting too close."

He turned and walked to the desk beneath the window.

"If you have a gun in that desk," Roxy said, "you better get it out quick."

She didn't know if there was one there, because she had never felt the need to check.

Gus shook his head and backed away from the desk, then turned and looked at Roxy.

"So it's over," he said. "It's kind of a relief."

"Let's go," Roxy told Gus. "We'll saddle a horse for you. There's a cell waiting back in Leadville. Stan, I'm guessing you'll be in charge for a while."

"Not me," Riley said. "I'm just the engineer. You tell Horace when you get back to put Richter in charge."

"Yeah, Richter," she said, thinking about the older man. They still had some unfinished business. "I'll tell him."

Coming in 2020!

Lady Gunsmith
9
Roxy Doyle and the Lady Executioner

For more information
visit: www.SpeakingVolumes.us

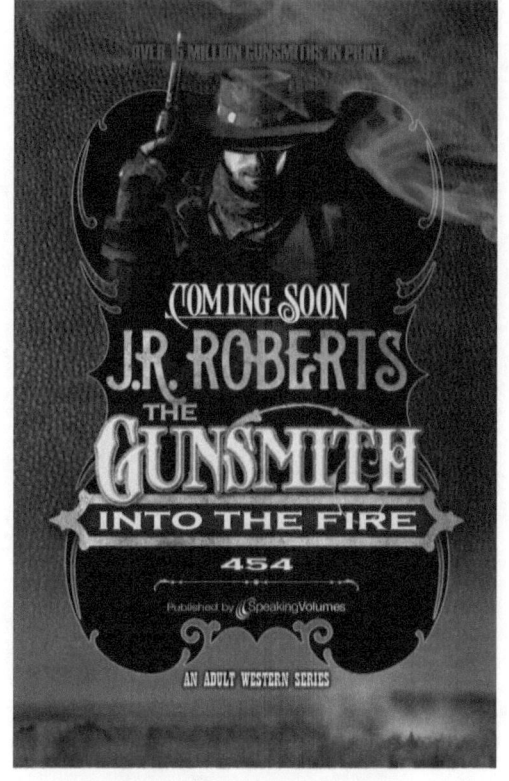

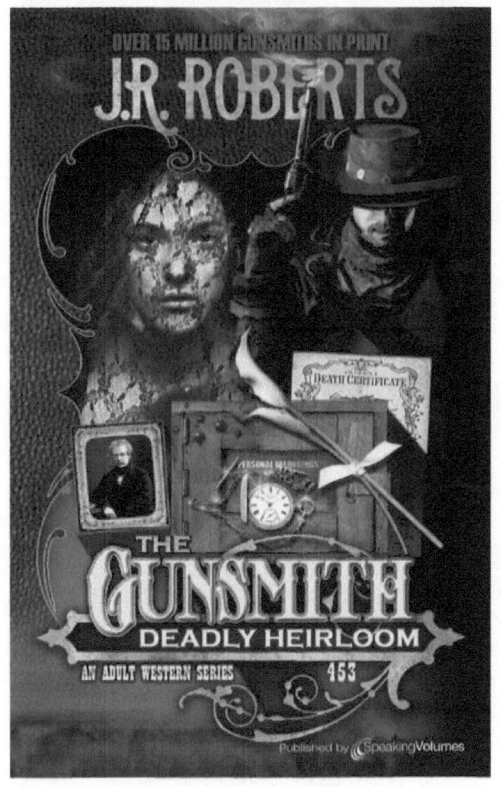

www.ingramcontent.com/pod-product-compliance
Lightning Source LLC
Chambersburg PA
CBHW032036240626
47154CB00003B/931
9781645401322